I0676962

SEX QUEEN

by

CHARLES NUETZEL

WRITING AS "STU RIVERS"

The Borgo Press
An Imprint of Wildside Press

MMVII

Dedicated to

Heidi,

A Dear Friend

SECOND EDITION

CONTENTS

INTRODUCTION

Sex Queen has an interesting history insofar as it involves a short event with Robert Bloch, who, among other things, was the author of the book *Psycho*, which Hitchcock made into the hit film by the same name.

I was at a party being given for professional writers by the editor of *Galaxy Science Fiction Magazine*, who was visiting Los Angeles at the time. Writers like Bloch and Ray Bradbury were among the guests.

We were all taking about, of all things, writing. For some reason I had the inspiration to share the statement that I was somewhat frustrated by the fact that I'd just finished this book, *Sex Queen*, in very short order. Robert Bloch's statement has stuck in my mind ever since: *the trouble with that is we tend to think we should be writing books at that same rate all the time!*

WOW! What a revelation. Sounds simple and obvious. But not really.

Which brings us back to the book itself. It was something that I actually very much enjoyed writing, dealing with characters that I had fairly well-rounded in my mind. Writers do tend to re-use plots and characters. Edgar Rice Burroughs admitted to having written the same book seventy times (more or less). So I'm not giving any confessional that isn't fairly common with most highly productive writers.

In any case, this book wrote itself, almost. I couldn't type fast enough. I couldn't keep away from the typewriter until I had finished it off in a fury of creative energy. (I refuse to admit for publication the exact length of time it took to do that first draft!)

Of course, there was a price-tag to pay for such a rapid pace of flushing words onto paper. That's a normal part of writing, too. A lot of times words won't come: the dreaded dry-spell. The fact is: you can squeeze the well quite dry. You need time to regenerate the flow and energies and the ideas.

But sometimes the ideas just race into your mind like a dam bursting apart and flooding the valley below. Your brain becomes overwhelmed and runs wild. Once the flood has ebbed away, it takes time to recharge itself. And that's the time of tortured hell.

If only a writer could continue racing from story to story, fanatically filling pages without stop. If I'd done that, I might have written one heck of a lot more stories, but at the same time I might have dropped dead from exhaustion many years ago.

Instead, we take our lingering moments of healing rest. And sometimes we even let ourselves embrace a long retirement from the demands of full-time writing.

But no matter what we might do, there are moments in our writing experience which stand out.

Sex Queen is the tragic story of one woman's descent and another's rise—the standard Hollywood story, told again and again. People come to town to seek stardom; all the lovely young people, eager for fame and riches. But those who make it seldom can keep it for very long.

This is a book that looks behind the scenes of the Hollywood glamour pit, and exposes some of the nightmares that fame and fortune can create for all the contenders for Hollywood Stardom.

—CHARLES NUETZEL
Thousand Oaks, California
August 2006

CHAPTER ONE

As Gale Ross watched her roommate slowly undress, she felt a hungry need begin to grow within her. It was a strange sensation, difficult to get used to. She still was stunned by the fact that they had become lovers. How odd and yet, how warmly friendly and welcomed in the icy world of Hollywood. There were plenty of men reaching out to use women, but that wasn't love; or comforting or desirable. One became even more isolated, and experienced a greater sense of being alone, unwanted, unneeded as a human being. And Gale was very needy; had been for almost a year.

And that had all worked to make her vulnerable to this woman's seductive intimacy. She let her eyes focus on Mildred's lovely body. The woman was simply amazing.

The pale moon flooded through the open window of their bedroom, caressing Mildred Mason's lush body as she slipped out of the gray skirt. She pulled her sweater over her head, revealing the heavy swell of her soft, fleshy breasts that were fighting against the tightly binding bra. She stared back, and her burning gaze ran over every inch of Gale's naked body.

Of the two women, Gale was by far the more beautiful. Her long blonde hair flowed over creamy white shoulders. Gale's generous lips dimpled every time she smiled. Her eyes of ocean blue reflected the innocence that remained of her childhood in a small Midwestern town.

"I still can't get over it," Mildred sighed, slipping down beside Gale. "You're the most beautiful woman I've ever known. I do love you..." Her fingers played lightly against Gale's breasts. "Yes, so beautiful..."

Gale tensed, feeling burning desire reach into the very depths of her, tightening the pink centers of her breasts.

She turned, lay back on the bed, and then stared invitingly up at Mildred.

The woman had heavy, lush breasts that were soft, warm cushions Gale loved to press against. The breasts were what had first attracted Gale. Later it had been the wonderful excitement of Mildred's love-making. Mildred knew how to make love, and create a romantic glow, a perfection that overshadowed the strange reality of Lesbian love.

They had met at one of the Hollywood parties. During their first conversation they learned how much alike they were, how they liked many of the same things. The following two weeks they had met at lunches and in the evenings, and finally decided to live together to cut expenses. It had been Mildred's idea, and Gale had jumped at it. Every thin dime saved allowed that much more money for make-up and dresses; the important weapons for a young struggling actress. Mildred had given up the idea of becoming an actress, but now devoted herself to help Gale in her stumbling attempts to success. When they first started living together nothing intimate had happened. Then one night, when they were alone, slightly high from several cocktails, they'd climbed into bed and suddenly made love in so natural a way that Gale never really knew how it had all come about. But it happened and now offered a strange meaning in her life: it filled a very real hunger to be needed as a human being, not a pound of flesh.

The affair had now lasted for several months and Gale was beginning to wonder if it would ever end. The thrill of Mildred, the soft, gentleness of the woman's love-making, had blurred all memory of how it was with a man. She had willingly fallen in with Lesbian love because it was so long since she had been possessed by a man. Since the loss of Wayne Gilman, over a year before, Gale's normal sexual hungers had no outlet. And she really didn't want to get involved with another man. The pain was still there. Mildred was the simple solution.

The loss of Wayne had been tragic for Gale. Wayne Gilman had just signed a contract at a major studio when the auto accident ended his life. What might have been the out-come to their romance, Gale would never know. She had dreamed of riding along on Wayne's career; giving up her own ambitions in favor of his. But all that ended on a week-end when he'd gotten too drunk to handle his car.

Now it was Mildred, because Gale didn't know a man who could replace Wayne and the tenderness that they had enjoyed. It had all been too perfect with him.

Gale suddenly realized why she was thinking

about Wayne, after all this time. Fourteen months of hectic living, ending up as a cocktail waitress for the *Chambers Steak House*, one of those expensive Hollywood diners that featured low lights, piano bar, privacy to stars, producers, and executives—a glamour stop-off for the tourist.

She was thinking about Wayne because the following day she had an appointment with the casting director of *Van Houten Pictures, Inc.* It was her first audition for over a year. Her new agent, Frankie Miller, had quickly landed a chance for a part in a television production. Mildred had introduced her to Frankie Miller three weeks before, in her campaign to promote Gale's career.

Slowly, as if coming out of a deep sleep, Gale found her attention wading out of the memories of the past and slipping back to the reality of the present.

Mildred's hands drifted lightly over Gale's stomach, across her breasts.

"You were thinking so hard, honey," Mildred said, "I was afraid you'd gone to sleep."

Gale reached for the woman, drawing her down close, pressing the softness of those hefty breasts against her own.

"Make love to me, Milly, please make love to me, don't let me think anymore. I don't want to think about anything...I just want to float on the thrill of your kisses...nothing else."

Mildred's large lips quickly covered Gale's. Their tongues blended together in rapid rhythm, their bodies closed tightly against one another.

Gale felt her breathing quicken; her lungs expand to the beat of their hearts pounding against each other.

Lesbian love was so different. Gale had felt awkward hesitation at the beginning. Her family would have been horrified to know what she experienced with Mildred. But then, her family would have been shocked to learn about her affair with Wayne. She came from a small town whose moral ideas were even smaller than the population of 18,000. Oh, there had been the wild parties, which the men's club threw once a month; but that was expected from men. The women of the town never, but never, talked about sex, and one would have thought they never even experienced it with their husbands.

Lesbian love didn't give the final gushing satisfaction that she longed for but it gave everything else, without the fears of being left with complications. In Lesbian love, Gale found a physical release for her pent up sexual desires. That didn't make it right in her mind; but, as far as she was concerned, it wasn't any more immoral than screwing around with any casting director, any producer or star who just "might" give her a hand up the ladder. The only hand those bastards generally gave was on the fanny. All in good sport. They were sports, all right; and they liked the game that was played with every starlet that came their way. Fun and games, no strings attached other than vague, empty promises. The egocentric bastards!

Her thoughts blurred for a moment, centering on the pleasure of Mildred's caressing hands and lips. The ecstasy well up like a gigantic wave of sensations, rolling over her again and again, each more wonderful. Then Gale laid back exhausted, her nerves slowly relaxing, her muscles unknotting in the aftermath of their love.

Tomorrow she was to see a man named Dan Blair. What kind of guy he was, she didn't know. She guessed he was probably some fat slob who would be all hands, all bug-eyes and hungry to discover if her breasts were real, if her hair was naturally blonde. A no-good slob, wanting to learn all there was about her; the intimate details—only.

"Nervous about tomorrow?" Mildred asked, lighting a cigarette and handing over the pack.

"Yes," Gale admitted, sitting up, striking a match to her cigarette and taking a deep drag.

"You shouldn't be, honey." Mildred patted her solidly firm thigh. "You've studied enough for the lead and this is just some bit part—hell. If anything you're over-qualified!"

"So I took several years of lessons, you know as well as I do that it takes more than that!" Gale snapped, irritated, and not knowing why she was so irritated.

"Oh, come on, I told you that Frankie has done favors for Van Houten. There's no reason to believe you won't get the part. It's nothing off Murry Van Houten's back. Frankie has put on the pressure...you know that." Mildred smiled, her wide lips opening over even white teeth that had been capped many years before, when she'd first decided on a Hollywood career. "Cheer up, honey, this is your first serious real big chance."

"I wonder what kind of guy this Dan Blair is?" Gale said thoughtfully, as if to herself.

"It doesn't matter. He'll be given orders from the top—and no matter what conditions he puts up—you just remember that! He'll probably try to bluff his way into your body. Don't, honey. Don't let that happen—he'll just be taking advantage of you. He's the casting director for the show, but...that's *all!* Van Houten gives the orders and that will be that!"

"What about Van Houten. I saw him at a party once with a couple of girls on his fat little shoulders. He..." Gale gagged slightly on the smoke. "Just thinking of letting him touch me...I don't think I could do that!"

Mildred embraced Gale, tenderly. "Silly. Frankie is in a position to see it doesn't happen. He discovered Holly—and I lined him up on something private—"

Gale tried to shake the thoughts from her head; but couldn't.

Morris Van Houten—Murry to the Hollywood set—was a gray-haired man in his early fifties, fat, red-faced, with a thin white mustache. He talked in all those show business sweethearts and darlings. And he played the women—all *the women!* It was rumored that he could manage as many as five a day. She doubted the truth of that statement. But he was known to throw large, wild parties at his huge Beverly Hills house that went on for a full weekend of booze, fun and games; with orgies that went on day and night, without end.

She realized that few people got anywhere in Hollywood without sleeping around at least with some power players. She would have to accept that fact, cold-bloodedly. And in the long run, she *would* accept it. A movie career had been one of her longest, and strongest desires. Even as a little girl, she'd haunted the magazine stand at *Turner's Drug Store,* buying the movie fan magazines the minute they came out. She read from cover to cover, until she knew every detail about every Hollywood personality. Until coming to Hollywood, a little over three years before, Gale believed what she had read. These three years had taught her one truth: not to believe *anything* she had read, would read, or did read about Hollywood. There were two sides to Hollywood; the side you read about and the side you learn about only if you were a part of it. Gale was to become part of it all.

Gale had promised herself, a long time ago, she didn't want to end up like Holly Hill, the Van Houten "Big Name" star. Holly Hill had slept her way to the top—and that meant with every stud along the way. No doubt she'd slept with so many guys that the mere number made it possible for her to get where she had aimed. Most women who did that ended as party-girls; or as just plain tramps, selling their bodies to any takers.

Gale hugged against Mildred, not wanting to think about the next day, only wanting to find escape in the soft warmth of the woman's body. She pressed her hand into the fullness of those large breasts, and then, suddenly, Mildred pulled her close and they stretched out, caressing, hugging, kissing, finding all the sensual areas that would rocket them into a world of ecstatic pleasure, where no thoughts, no dreams, no ambitions could touch them.

And in that world, Gale found the temporary escape she so hungrily needed.

Afterwards, lying in the darkness, Gale found

16

herself worrying again. Some time later, she got up, went into the kitchen, found the bottle of whiskey they had opened earlier in the evening, and poured herself a stiff shot. Downing it in one quick swallow, Gale stood there, looking through the kitchen window, across the town which stretched out toward the Hollywood hills.

How many people had looked into the Hollywood night, seeing the heavenly stars, and wished for themselves the fantasy that finally made them into movie stars? She wondered.

The Garbos, the Gables, the Valentinos, and Monroes: all of them struggling and making it to the top. They had all hugged their dreams close to themselves, and then reached out and grabbed what was necessary to make it happen.

Even the Holly Hills.

Would she be one of them? Would the price be worth it?

Gale wondered, knowing that tomorrow would be her first real chance to find out. Until now she'd merely played at the game. She had taken the dramatic lessons, she had acted in amateur plays, she had run around the outer fringes of the Hollywood set, but had never actually reached that point where her chance for even a walk-on came about. The interviews of the past had ended quickly when the men attempted to get her into bed. With Wayne Gilman, she had fallen in love, had an affair, and let her so-called career simmer down, while taking the dramatic lessons, and continuing to hold the dreams. Then his death had changed things and for a while she had simply drifted from day to day. Then Mildred came with her offerings.

17

Pouring another shot of whiskey, Gale stared at it for a moment and then gulped it down.

Before Hollywood she didn't drink so much. But drinking had become part of it, too. And she liked to drink, Gale realized. In the past months, with Mildred, she'd done a lot of drinking. Since getting Frankie Miller as an agent, Gale had turned to the bottle even more.

Was that going to be part of the price, too?

Maybe, maybe, she admitted. But no drugs!

She would try, try hard to get there, and if the price became too high, she'd even try paying it, without bitching to herself or feeling self-pity.

The last years had taught her the bitter lesson: idealism was dead; reality demanded full payment for any pay-offs.

Returning to the bedroom, Gale looked down at her roommate.

How attractive Mildred looked. Even for a hefty woman, Mildred was extremely attractive.

But how long could this affair last? Gale asked herself. It had begun because she needed an outlet; both physical and emotional. Yet it couldn't last forever. She wanted real love; a romance that led somewhere other than a Lesbian orgasm. It had been so beautiful with Wayne. Now she craved the real thing to happen again. Only, she hadn't met a man who could match up to Wayne. And doubted she ever would. So, horrible as it sounded even to her own mind, Mildred was better than nothing. And, quite frankly, very good at seducing her. At least she had this to cling to. A slim straw in a raging storm.

The two drinks suddenly reached up to her head,

caressing gently, murmuring sleep to her.

Gale slipped under the covers, and after a short time sleep settled over the whispering thoughts, giving them rest.

CHAPTER TWO

Dan Blair opened the door for his date, and they stepped into his plush Hollywood apartment.

Helen Biggs, cute little secretary to Murry Van Houten, wiggled her way across the darkened room to the large windows that overlooked Hollywood, which was stretched out below.

"I never tire of that sight, Danny," she squealed delightedly. Her voice was high, and slightly slurred from the flow of drinks that had gone down her tiny white throat.

Dan slowly closed the door behind him, his hand hesitated at the light switch and then fell away.

He watched the dark shadow of the redheaded secretary come to a stop at the sofa in front of the window. He heard shoes clatter to floor as Helen climbed onto the sofa and looked out the window that offered a view of the endless expanse of colorful lights stretched out like strings of jewels: Hollywood at night.

Dan's head was spinning slightly and his nerves were tired from the long, exhausting day at the office. He was casting the *Henderson City Story,* a new television series about newspaper work in a small city. That afternoon Van Houten had called his office to say that a Gale Ross would be coming in at one the next day for an interview and that he was to use her in some bit part—because some agent, to whom Murry owed a favor, was pushing her. That was all Dan needed. The day had been hectic enough without orders from the top telling him how to cast his show. Van Houten knew how he felt about such things, but that didn't make a damned difference.

Helen's voice cut his thoughts in half.

"You going to stand their all night?" she asked.

Dan looked across the room at her silhouette. Helen had turned, so that her thrusting bust line profiled against the background. She had a pert little figure, into which every guy on the lot had sent his greetings. But she was good; and a lot of fun. Helen didn't think about anything serious. She merely let men take her out, and expected to end up in an apartment, motel; a bed. She was basic sex, and didn't mind showing it. That's why Van Houten had her as a secretary. When there wasn't some other broad to fill the bill for a boring afternoon, Murry Van Houten called in his little secretary, closed and locked the office door and whiled away half an hour in party games.

"Well, Danny?" Helen inquired, putting hands under the curve of her breasts. "Wanna go for them? I didn't come up here to merely play staring games—and across the room at that!"

Dan laughed and walked to her.

She eagerly came into his arms. Her lips turned up under his. They were small lips, but soft, yielding and moist. In the semi-darkness, their surface was outline, bright.

21

"Kiss me, Danny...kiss me. I've waited long enough. That party was the dullest!" She wiggled against him, and slipped her arms around his waist. "Hug me tight, Danny. You're strong. I like you. I've always liked you a lot, Danny."

She was some kid; a crazy bundle of sexual energy. And kinda funny.

Her bright, deep blue eyes, sparkling in the darkness, were anxious, and almost childlike.

He wondered why she'd ended up as she was. Of course, Helen had a powerful sex urge; and that was part of the explanation. No one man could ultimately keep up with her.

She pressed greedily against him as their lips hungrily opened to a heated kiss.

How many girls had he taken to his apartment like this young throbbing ball of womanhood? He'd lost count. It seemed an endless, meaningless procession of female flesh. Yet he was single, enjoying a wonderfully full life with plenty of female companionship on call any day or night. Helen was just one of many casual intimate interludes.

When they broke away, Helen laughed, nervously.

"It was a dull party, wasn't it?" Helen asked, reaching around to the back of her dress to unzip it. Her eyes looked up into his. "Why don't you fix us a drink? While I get ready."

As if she needed to get ready; she was always ready.

Before he could make any objection, Helen wiggled herself away, across the living room, stumbling over a footstool, and then to the bedroom doorway. She hesitated long enough to finally slip the zipper down her back and let the cloth fall to the floor. Turning, she blew a kiss toward him.

"Hurry, Danny," she whispered, disappearing into the room. "I'm hot all over!"

As Dan mixed straight rum and brandy, he thought about the party which had been so "dull."

Actually, from his point of view, it hadn't been too bad. But for a "Hollywood" party, which meant to Helen Biggs, a Van Houten or Holly Hill all-out orgy, it'd been dullsville. The cocktails had flowed like water, but the crowds milled in dull conversation. He had managed a few new contacts, which might pan out sometime in the future. He didn't want to remain a casting director all his life. His conversation with Jack Davis, an independent producer, had indicated that the large, beady-eyed man was looking for a director for his latest quickie movie. When Dan had indicated his own interest in directing, Davis told him that maybe they might work out something. But that would be some months in the future. The idea intrigued him. The conversation had bored Helen enough so that she'd left for another cocktail before the interesting parts had been exchanged. But she soon returned to continually squeeze his arm, suggestively, and whisper in his ear invitations to an all-night delivery of hot sex.

"Danny...D-a-n-n-y!" Helen's pixie voice called from the bedroom.

"Okay!" he answered, picking up the two glasses. He walked to the bedroom.

Helen was lying on the bed, the covers just hiding the most desirable portion of her body, but revealing the pert little swell of her breasts. They were

23

nicely shaped breasts, with dark pink mounting their tips. She was breathing lightly; the actions caused her breasts to rise and gently fall, taunting him.

He sat down beside her and handed her the drink. She rose up on one elbow, sipping from the glass.

"Gad—what the hell is it?" She made a face. Her turned up nose wrinkled, her lips pursed up tight.

"Rum and brandy."

"You getting me drunk?" she accused. "Think you need to get me drunk to tickle my fancy…down there?"

He laughed, slipped his hand under the covers, caressing her.

She yelped and grinned. "You bastard! Can't you wait until a girl is drunk to say it was the booze, not your wonderful charming, sexy self that seduced her?"

"That's what you wanted, isn't it?" he inquired, withdrawing his hand.

"Yes—but…" She sipped the drink again, and made a repeat performance of the face. "That's strong! Is that a promise that you'll be as strong?"

"You're a strong girl," he countered, grinning.

"What does that mean?" She frowned this time.

"You have strong appetites—in men," he observed, eyeing her cupid breasts.

"You beast!" She wiggled and her breasts danced. "What makes you so talkative? I don't want conversation."

"I thought we came up here for conversation," he said, amused.

"Conversation? Maybe that's what you call it—

but I call it sex!"

"Sex is physical conversation." He played with the tip of her breast and then caressed her stomach.

"Where'd you hear that?" she murmured, kissing his cheek.

"Elliott."

"Elliott Wood is a..."

"Watch what you say, lover," he warned, pulling her close; their lips were only inches apart.

"Oh, you know I like Elliott...but he's...well, with his...writing..." She smothered the words against his mouth and then coyly pushed him back: "You know he writes sex novels?"

"So?"

"He dedicated one to me. Said I was the main character. You should have seen what kind of girl he made me! Boy—I wish I could get that many men—that *kind* of men. They do it all night, without stop! Boy—the creeps I've bedded with. They couldn't manage one time a night—and some of them go limp before they get big enough to enjoy my fancy!"

"That's a hell of a thing to say," he moaned, staring in mocked amazement at her.

"Oh, they aren't *all* like that. But..." She giggled, and winked over the rim of the glass at him and then giggled again. "The other night...boy— what a character *that* guy was!" She sipped her drink, giggled again. "Some creep in the art department...forgot his name. But at that party Holly gave...well, we ended up—as I always like to end up—but he was...hell, he couldn't finish the first act...*boy*—what a disappointment.. All muscle, wavy blonde hair and a low, throaty voice—what a hash that night was."

"Carl Fern?" Dan asked.

"Yeah...how'd you know?"

"He'd rather be with big boys!" he told her.

Helen almost choked on her drink. Her eyes grew large, her mouth burst with a gurgling sound. "Oh, gad—me with a...well one of those guys? That's a real...yucky laugh!"

"Well, he tries. All screwed up. Thought you knew about him." Dan eyed her breasts, suddenly getting tired of the verbal conversation.

"Danny, I shan't know...hey! Happy shime! I'm shrunk!" She threw her glass across the bed the contents spilled on the covers, and flung her arms around his neck.

There wasn't any time to think about the wet bed. The verbal conversation had abruptly come to a heated end.

The kiss bore deep, each of them taking turns tasting the depths of the other's mouths. He pressed his hand into the small swell of her breast, which barely filled his palm. Her body trembled as they fell slowly back against the bed.

After a moment Dan got up, quickly undressed and then returned, slipping under the covers.

She squirmed close to him, her warm little body pressing anxiously against his.

"You're good, Danny," she murmured wiggling even closer. Her lips closed around the lobe of his ear and her tongue played lightly, as he enjoyed the feel of her breast.

It was a long time before they shifted, so that he could have complete freedom to explore the length of her body. She trembled under his kisses, her eyes

26

clamped tightly together, her fingers dug into his back. Soft purring moans sounded from her throat.

He made love to her automatically, as he'd done so many times in the past, to her and to so many other women.

Dan kept feeling a vague sense of emptiness, as if he'd been there before, too many times. It had nothing to do with the excitement his body was feeling, nothing to do with the normal, animal need which had to find some outlet; it was merely an empty feeling that all this was getting him nowhere, fast. Been there; done that.

When he had first started in the Hollywood game, as an extra, finally ending up as casting director for the Van Houten Studios, the idea of having a "harem" of seductive women with whom to play midnight games, seemed fantastically attractive. That had been some ten years before, when he was young enough to know very little about women. He'd managed a couple of affairs, and the normal amount of teenage exploration earlier, but nothing like what he dreamed would come in the future.

After a couple of years knocking around as an extra, going to the endless parties, making endless, useless contacts, he had decided to settle for something less glamorous, and work his way up into directing. It had taken seven years of hard work to get to his present position as casting director, escaping the sensual hands of both the gays and the nympho ladies of the Industry. But the women had gotten their fair attention, and he'd managed to set himself up in a plush, fancy office where young starlets were willing to spread all the feminine goodies on the sacrificial table of "help-me-with-my-career."

For a long while he'd enjoyed all the wild young goodies, as any man in his position might. The only thing that had seemed pointless was the infinity of young things willing to serve banquets of "love" for a mere chance at getting a part. How many women he'd possessed in long train-ride to nowhere, he didn't know. But there had been many, and all beautiful beyond any wild dreams of an "Arabian Nights" Sultan. And they had come in so many different shapes and sizes and desires. And all more than willing to offer themselves up on the casting couch as a career move.

One, he remembered, was a woman he'd been forced, by circumstances, to seduce, in order to get the present position. Ruth Gordon, a tall, broad shouldered, narrow faced bitch who liked her night-meals served with a lot of spicy sadism. The only thing was that this woman liked too much grossed out seasoning. If a man didn't hit her face, and real hard, at the very moment of physical union, she got nothing from the exercise. She had a hard face, and a greedy appetite. Those long nights, when he'd been forced to continue the perverse affair, had taught him one hell of a lot about the masochistic female. The spankings, which had left her fanny red, raw, were only the beginnings of their erotic nights adventures.

At least Helen Biggs wasn't like that.

Helen surged up against him, a deep throated moan gurgling from her trembling mouth.

In those final moments, Dan's mind went black, his nerves burned raw. His pulse quickened. His breathing became heavy and perspiration rolled from his brow. She easily totally drained a man.

28

With a sigh, Dan fell away from the woman, lying on his back next to her.

Helen was a little wild lady in heat. Not much more. A good little girl for a quick party. Any time, any place. Call up, pick up; knock down for a wild evening of games.

Helen, the body that launched a thousand men into action. Probably more than a thousand.

He turned and looked at Helen, wondering what made a woman live her kind of life. Where would she end? Some hospital before her time, sick and spent out. A nowhere girl, riding a nowhere rocket, to nowhere but a sad fizzle. A fiery tail assembly, burning too bright, too fast, burning out in the atmosphere. Finished. Red-hot mamma convulsing in the last moments of existence. And for what? Nothing. A complete waste. How much money, how much love, dreams, had her parents put into her? Their little girl ending as everybody's little girl. It was sad. And depressing.

Dan had never thought of it that way. Those girls, all those girls, struggling to reach the top, and ending on the bottom. What were the parents like? Not all of the parents were decent members of society, but enough were. And their daughters? Like Helen? Or worse? Helen knew what she was; she didn't try to fool herself or others. In some ways a free spirit, swinging through life without much thought other than the momentary pleasures. Some people were like that. Regardless of their sexual leanings. Others were more focused. But what about the girls who did fool themselves? They were the pitiful ones. Talent? Hell, the only talent most of them had was the ability to let a man find his pleasure in the night-meals they could offer.

What a terrible shame.

"Helen, where are you going?" he found himself asking, surprised by his own question.

The woman sat up, frowning, looking down at him with amazement in her eyes.

"What kind of question is that?" she demanded, her pixie face screwed up.

"Just a silly one," he said, looking away.

A long silence settled between them and the only sound was the night noise of the city. A murmuring of silence in the dark night, nothing more. Maybe the wind moaning, maybe the soft distant rustle of traffic; or the multiple sighs of a million lovers finding the mystery of life.

How many lovers, real lovers, found meaning in their physical experience with one another; a meaning that came from love and emotional feeling, not just from sexual need?

He wondered what it was like.

Dan had forgotten that some time in the last ten years. Forgotten in the drowning surge of too much willing female flesh. He had been in love, once. A girl named Joan…something. *Funny,* he thought, *he couldn't remember her last name.* But they had been very much in love. And they had loved for a beautiful summer; a hot, violent summer that had consumed their whole beings. Then she'd suddenly gotten ill. They said it was a cold, but "they"—whoever they were—were wrong. She died so fast; too fast. Hope—and then death. It had taken a long time, and a lot out of him, to forget. Now, Dan realized, he had forgotten. Maybe too well.

Too many in-between; too many to count; too

many that didn't count—emotionally.

Once more he turned and looked at the woman next to him.

Dear little Helen—office hellion! Cute, little pixie Helen Biggs, who probably didn't have the brains to know what she really wanted out of life— or enough brains to realize that she *should* want something out of life. Maybe the Helen Biggses were happier. They didn't think; they didn't have the mental material to think beyond the moment, beyond the instant of physical need. Sleep, eat, sex. Simple, in any order that it might come up.

Who knows, maybe less torment and more pleasure was a desirable place to live life. Some could; like Helen did. They lived, enjoyed and after a while died. Maybe that's all their lives were meant to be.

Yet, perhaps even Helen had managed to few tragic love affairs. Maybe it had been the hurt of some lost lover that had made her the way she was. Maybe a man had hurt her, and left her, and she'd merely gone off, much like himself, seeking out any man, all men, to soothe away the hurt memory, and finally she'd learned how to *not* feel, or think or care about thinking or feeling.

Gently, as if he almost understood, still embraced in his make-believe fantasy about Helen, Dan reached for her. He pulled her close, tenderly, as a lover might, as maybe her lost lover had, caring, trying to care and understand. Maybe trying to find the feeling that had left him so long ago when his Joan had suddenly found there wasn't any life in her.

His lips touched Helen's, lightly, attempting to

feel the real depth of this little creature.

But she wiggled, her mouth opened, her tongue danced brazenly into his mouth, uncaring, unfeeling, automatically seeking out the sensual thrill of the moment, the wild erotic stimulation designed to rocket her through a speedy accent into the blackness of starry space. Then to fall back in the thick cool atmosphere, and burn up.

And the dream-fantasy broke, shattered, and he was merely loving a sexual machine who wanted the right buttons to be pushed in order to create the wild erotic reaction she so mindlessly craved.

He pushed the buttons, automatically, as he realized he always did, with one small portion of his mind aware of the mockery of what was happening. For a short while that mocking laughed in his ears, until the physical hungers overcame the laughter and drowned it out in a sputtering explosion of electric pleasure. The joint rocket soared into the heavens, saw the brightness of the Milky Way and then dropped downwards into flaming heat that completely consumed its being, breaking it apart in a final convulsion of hunger, leaving nothing but raw nerve endings to soothe away in exhausted sleep.

When he awoke the sun was streaming through the bedroom window, shining across his face. Someday, he thought, he would have to move the bed.

Helen was already up, starting to pull her bra over the neat little swells of her still youthful breasts.

She smiled down at him.

"Time to go to work, Danny," she announced, hooking her bra strap. Then she bounced back to the bed.

She leaned over and kissed his lips. "You were sure a lot of fun," she laughed brightly. "A real ball! Or two!"

Sighing, Dan got up to another day; another day in a long series of days that had become a mere automatic habit.

He wondered who it would be tonight; what woman would share his bed into the long hours of the next morning.

Maybe it would be this Gale something-or-other he was supposed to give a bit part to. Maybe he could con her into an evening of meaningless sexual exercise. Or maybe she would turn out to be something better? Sure. Of course. Just like all the others.

What a dream that was! he thought, getting up and walking into the bathroom. *A mocking dream that had questioned itself into existence every morning at this same time. A dream which never came true.*

Dan looked at himself in the mirror and groaned.

His handsome features were haggard looking, the squared jaw a little too square, the dark wavy hair mussed up over his forehead.

There you are, you aimless bastard, he thought picking up his electric razor. *There you are, getting a little older, getting a little more tired, getting a little more disillusioned about life and women and everything. Everything in the whole goddamned world!*

His head throbbed with a hangover and continued to throb as he slipped into his car next to Helen.

The day was sunny, but his mood, as always,

was gray and overcast.

Maybe, someday in the near distant future, Jack Davis would give him a break and let him direct a z-class quickie. Maybe that would make things worth the effort. There wasn't any other reason to look forward to the future. Certainly not women like Helen Biggs, and all the other broads that served night-meals. He was desperately hungry for some else, brighter, fuller, more meaningful. Life had become routine and dulled.

He sighed and paid attention to driving along the curving road down the Hollywood hills, toward *Van Houten Studios.*

CHAPTER THREE

Gale had dressed in a green sheath that showed off enough of her figure to invite a man's eye, but not his hand. The soft cloth hugged her upswept, full breasts. It was cut low at the top to reveal the swell of creamy white flesh; it hugged her waist and flared out to caress her rounded hips, bleeding off, along her firm thighs, just hinting at their fullness.

As she walked into the office marked, DAN BLAIR, CASTING DIRECTOR, Gale fought down the nervous swarm of butterflies dancing along the lining of her stomach.

The office was outwardly plain, at first glance, with a modern desk at one side, several overstuffed leather chairs and a magazine rack, with a planter that held fake greenery lining the walls. The carpet was thick and yielding under her high heeled shoes.

A regal looking young woman sat behind the desk, her chestnut brown hair done up on top of her head, Roman-style. Her eyes were shadowed in blue, her brows high, arching, her lips wide, full, red. The figure that showed above the desk top looked attractively lush, but classy. The woman glanced up and smiled in that warm impersonal way studio secretaries had perfected down to a fine art: it

35

said the boss wasn't available, unless you have an appointment.

"Yes?" the woman asked in a cultured, controlled voice.

"Doris Patton?" Gale inquired, determined not to be put down by this woman's professional manner. No doubt she was making points with her boss; a little lady playing bed-games, no doubt. "I'm Miss Ross. Mr. Blair has an appointment with me."

That was reversing the reality, since she was the one who had an appointment with him.

Doris Patton's expression grew serious as she looked at an appointment pad on her desk. She seemed to take more time than it was necessary to find Gale's name.

"You're *Gale* Ross?" she finally asked, not looking up from the notepad. "A Mr. Miller sent you?"

"Yes," Gale admitted, holding back a quick retort. The little bitch knew exactly who she was.

"Will you wait for a moment, Mr. Blair is busy right now," Doris Patton announced. Her eyes snapped toward the chairs. "Might sit down, it'll be a while." Her smile was professional again. After a full minute, she returned her attention to the desk top, apparently busy reading the open folder.

Gale walked to the nearest chair, picked up a copy of the latest Time, and thumbed through it.

Nervousness edged up through her. With every moment she felt sharp pangs edge all over her body. What could be taking so long? The appointment was for one o'clock. What could he be doing in there? Didn't the bastard go out to lunch?

It was the same old game of waiting. Wait for a

quick interview that would get you nowhere.

Didn't even a Frankie Miller count? she wondered, turning a page, and looking at the face of an old, wrinkled man. She studied the face for a long time, and then turned the page again.

"Miss Ross...you can go in, now," Doris Patton's voice called.

Gale looked up. She hadn't heard anybody leave the office. Had they slipped by without her noticing? That seemed impossible. Maybe there was another entrance to the office, and the person had gone out that way. Gale stood, carefully put the magazine on the table next to the chair. She turned, then heard the magazine fall to the floor. Hurriedly she bent over and picked it up. When she turned toward the inner office door, it was open and a tall, good looking man was staring at her. His brown eyes were twinkling, almost laughing. His lips were nicely shaped, especially while smiling.

"Miss Ross?" he said in a low, pleasant voice.

"Yes," she admitted, feeling a flush rush up her face.

He'd been giving her fanny a real once over. The dirty little bugger.

Her eyes went over the man's trim, solid looking body. He was wearing an expensive blue-gray suit that fit perfectly. It must have put him back a bundle. No doubt he could afford that—then write if off as a business expense. She walked across the short space between them, and past the man who held open the door for her.

"Sit down, Miss Ross," he invited, moving around his large, oak desk, and settling down in the swivel chair. He studied her as she tried to relax in the over-comfortable chair opposite him. "A Mr. Miller sent you, didn't he?"

She tried to watch the bridge of his nose. It was a trick she'd learned. When you looked at the bridge of a person's nose they couldn't tell you weren't looking directly into their eyes. But it wasn't to fool him, it wasn't to make herself look relaxed, and un-ruffled, but to keep from feeling the sudden surge of physical attraction that whipped the stomach butter-flies into revolt. He was one hell of a damned good looking man. Not what she'd expected at all. He couldn't be over thirty-five—if that; and he was at least six feet two, in height.

"Miss Ross..." he said, leaning forward, peering into her eyes. "Mr. Miller sent you, didn't he?"

She shook her head and tried to smile.

"I'm sorry." A flush rushed to her cheeks. "Yes."

He tapped a cigarette on the edge of the desk, without offering her one. Then he lighted it, casu-ally. All the time his eyes were impersonally study-ing her.

"Tell me, can you act?" he inquired in an even voice, as if he didn't believe she could do anything but make bed-games.

"I've had some experience," Gale told him icily. Then quickly added, the flush turning deeper red, burning her cheeks: "In acting."

He smiled and then dragged deeply on his ciga-rette. "You're attractive."

"Thanks for nothing!" She got a cigarette from her purse. He leaned over the desk to light it for her. For an instant their eyes met, his probing, hers nerv-ously wanting to look away, but not able to. He seemed to be looking for her soul.

"What you done?" Dan Blair inquired, leaning back, relaxing in the chair. "What experience do you have?"

Damned him, she thought, *he's so casual, so relaxed and calm, and I'm sweating—really sweating. Just like a bull-necked truck driver.*

"Well, didn't Mr. Miller tell Murry all there was to tell?" she countered, hoping the bluff would work. The use of Mr. Van Houten's first name should snow him good, she told herself.

"Not enough. Even if the part's simple—we don't like rank amateurs holding up production while they *learn* how to act. Regardless of what you might think about the Industry, we don't have time to be an acting school for young hopefuls. And as you must—"

"I understand that," she interrupted, icily, holding the edge of the chair with her right hand, trying to fight back the nasty retort threatening to spit out at him. "I've been around long enough, Mr. Blair, to know the score. I hope you understand that."

The change his face made at her words caused Gale to regret them. Maybe her tone had been a little too harsh, her words a little too biting.

He frowned for a moment and then let out a long, deep sigh.

"You understand it's just a walk-on part?" he finally said, hardly looking at her. "A very few lines."

"I think we all have to start at the bottom, don't we?"

"Yes." He fingered a letter opener, flipped it around in his hands and then looked up at her again. His eyes were probing, deeper this time. "Leave your name with my secretary...we'll call you."

He stood and stepped around the desk.

For a moment she sat there, numbed, the anger flushed up over her whole body. So this was it? The brush off! Even with a personal contact. Even with everything in her favor.

Standing, she glared up at the man who had stopped only a foot away.

"I was told that Mr. Van Houten would see that I got the part—what right does a little snot like you have to give me the brush off! Do you know how hard a girl struggles—and the kinds of slobs that try to get in her way! Damn you and damned all of the shits like you!" Her hands were clawed against her thighs, her eyes flaring hatred into his. "What the hell right do men like you have to stand in the way of an honest girl trying to—"

"Hold on! *Hold on!*" Dan Blair cried, flinging his arms in the air, his voice on the verge of laughing. "I'm sorry. Really..."

"Sorry about what? What is there to be sorry about, Mister Blair? The Big All-Mighty Blair—who just says—"

"You'll have the part!"

"—that this woman doesn't get the part and—"

"You have the part!" he yelled over her, laughter in his eyes.

He reached out, touched her.

The air crackled. Electricity flared between them; bounced all over the room, as if lightning had struck.

Gale jumped away from the man's hand, staring at him as if physically shocked by an electric bolt.

He jerked back, his face drawn serious, his

mouth hanging open, his dark large eyes wide, open amazement in complete control of their very depths.

For a long eternity they stood there, numbed.

"Wow!" he breathed after a moment, his wide shoulders relaxing, his hands dropping to his side. "What happened?"

She shook her head and looked away, biting on her lower lip. For a long time she was too dazed to say anything.

Then she shook off the surprise and forced her voice into control, said: "I get the part?"

The tone, the quality of the tremor, surprised Gale. She was shaking and not knowing why. Suddenly she needed a drink.

In a daze, without realizing what she was doing, Gale walked out of the office, not saying a word, past the secretary, without leaving her phone number with the woman. She kept walking until she was standing in front of the Ford she had bought a couple of years before.

Still dazed, Gale got into the car, started the engine and drove out of the Studio parking lot. At the first bar she stopped, got a Martini. Thirty minutes later she was still sitting at the bar stool, looking at the empty glass, idly fingering the dry olive.

She didn't know whether to be more surprised at having got the part, after the seeming "brush-off," or the reaction to his touch.

Dan Blair was one hell of a man; that much she couldn't help admitting. Just the kind of male animal any girl would fall all over herself to attract.

It was the first time she'd ever experienced such a reaction from a mere touch. If that was what it was?

Maybe an accident.

Then she thought about his handsome features, his solid, tall body, and his dark brown eyes that had probed so deeply into hers, his low, resilient voice. A strange exciting thrill flushed over her.

Noticing the empty glass, she ate the olive and ordered a second cocktail.

Half an hour later she was still sitting there, staring at another empty glass, fingering another dry green olive, thinking about Dan Blair and trying to puzzle out her reaction to him, his touch and the fact that she had gotten the part.

But most of all: what a delicious dish of a male animal he was!

CHAPTER FOUR

"I don't care what you think," the heavy, gross Morris "Murry" Van Houten was saying to Dan, "I don't care about anything except getting Holly Hill soothed. You insulted her somehow—now you got to do something about it!"

Dan just stood there in the large office, staring at his boss, still unable to believe what he had heard.

"Damn it, Murry, what she have in for me? I never even—hell, I'm just one of the help to her, and—"

Van Houten stabbed the air with his cigar, said:

"Look, sweetheart, I don't know what's going on in that woman's head. Who *does* know? For some damned reason she wants you at her home tonight—and you better make sure you play up to her."

Dan sighed, feeling sickness ebb through him. "Nothing happened—Murry. Hell, it was last weekend—I'd almost forgotten, and she...well, I guess she made a pass at me—"

"And you turned her down?" Van Houten demanded, amazement making his voice even raspier. "Look, sweetheart, when a Holly Hill makes a pass at a guy—he doesn't turn her down! He gulps it

43

whole! She's getting to that age where she wants lovers—on command—and now...well, she says you apologize, or she wants you out of the studio. Now, you and me know that's silly—but she's serious and we need a Holly Hill more than we need a Dan Blair. Understand?" The cigar stabbed the air again, and Van Houten wiped his sweating forehead with the back of his hand. "Look, sweetheart, just do what she wants—so...what's wrong with a little private party...? And she's still a hot lady. But she wants to be convinced she's still the lovely sex-pot of five years back. Women hitting mid-thirty get funny—and she's already well past that mark! By maybe a decade for all I know."

Dan shrugged, trying to figure how he'd managed to "insult" Holly Hill so terribly that she'd make such a fuss out of nothing. It had been last weekend, at one of her blast-outs.

"What happened, anyway," Van Houten demanded, plunking down in his large chair.

"Oh, I was at the bar, you know, outside on the patio, with Jean Temple—and Holly came up, making with the sexy stuff. You know, her standard stuff."

Van Houten laughed, knowingly. "A wiggle here and a bounce there? A bit of the bending over to reveal her boobies are big and large and fully packed? That kind of stuff?"

"Something like that. I merely thought she was kidding when she suggested we go away to one of her private rooms—hell, I was with Jean...I couldn't drop Jean for Holly and—"

"God, oh, God, Sweetheart...what you did what you did! What's with you, kid? Don't you know the

SEX QUEEN, BY CHARLES NUETZEL

first thing about women? You turn down THE Holly Hill for some kid half her age...what'd you expect?" Van Houten slowly shook his massive head from side to side, his white hair looked like a fringe around the pink bald spot. His fat features, already red, seemed to darken to deep crimson.

"Sweetheart...you go out there tonight, and you make love to Holly like you never made love to nobody in your ever-loving life. You kissy-kissy every inch of her stacked boobs and every inch of the rest of her until she screams in delight! And that's an order. You soothe that steak-house of feminine flesh until she cries uncle—you do that...or so help me I'll blow the whole show off the road—everything will go...you won't be able to get a job anywhere in Hollywood! You plant yourself on her bod and you make love like you never made love before—and you don't stop fucking she until begs you to stop! You make her think the sun sets with her, the moon rises with her...you make her believe you...and you calm her down—you do that, sweetheart...you do that for Daddy Van Houten...and I don't have no more headaches." He slapped his forehead as if in agony, and rolled his eyes to the ceiling. "As if the good Lord didn't give me enough trouble...now this young healthy stud makes a fool out of the most lovely, sweet little woman this side of heaven."

Dan fought down the nausea, bit hard on his cigarette and tried to ignore the endless ranting that raged from Van Houten.

Suddenly the big man broke off from his heavenly ravings, and turned beady eyes at Dan.

"You lay that bitch ten to one—and you lay her good. I don't want any more trouble from the slut!

You hear me, Dan? You hear me?" Van Houten stood, glaring down at him.

Dan groaned inwardly and stood. He forced a grin.

"The pleasure's mine, Murry."

Murry Van Houten's face moved from hard stone to soft, flabby grinning flesh. His eyes grew little, wrinkling up at the corners, his pug-nose flared slightly, and his lips spread wide over the corn teeth. "You're a good guy, Danny-boy...you won't be sorry for this, believe me."

Van Houten slapped Dan's back. "I know this wasn't your fault. Hell, who can out-guess a woman like Holly? You just gotta try; grease the breast a little. Hell, she just wants a little loving. What man—what man in the whole United States—hell, in the whole world, wouldn't like to be in your position? Every young stud, from ten to a hundred, would give his right nut to party with Holly Hill. The sex dream of a century. Holly Hill, begging to have a guy spend the night with her. That's all she wants. Just a little lovin'! Who doesn't want love? The whole world turns on love. We dish it out to them with the Holly Hills of this town. She gives of herself—and what does she ask in return? Just a little love in return. That's all she wants. Just a little lost girl, who doesn't think she's loved. I envy you, Danny-boy...I envy you...every man in America envies you. Holly Hill—every man's dream of a love-mate. And she's turning the whole studio in-side-out, just because she wants you. Just imagine!"

All the time he headed Dan toward the door. "You're a lucky stud. And I expect you to stud her right, left and down the middle...make a deep impression…if you get my meaning, my boy!"

He opened the door for Dan and finished off with:

"You're lucky, Danny-boy...a real lucky.... Do this favor and you won't be sorry. Just get her off my back. Gotta keep my people happy, ya know. And Holly has hills to be explored and …"

The door slammed behind Dan and he leaned against it for a moment, still dazed.

"What happened?" Helen Biggs asked, looking up from her desk.

"You wouldn't guess in a million years," Dan moaned.

"I know it's something about you and Holly." Her eyes twinkled, teasingly.

Dan just walked out and returned to his office.

Elliott Wood was waiting.

Without a word, Dan grabbed Elliott's arm, directed him down the hall, toward the entrance to the studio building.

"Hey, where're you taking me?" Elliott cried, jerking his arm away.

"A drink."

"Suits me fine," Elliott conceded, grinning. "But why the silence?"

They walked outside into the afternoon heat.

"Tell you later...sometime after a couple of Martinis. What's it you want, Elliott?" Dan asked, turning and looking at the man.

Elliott Wood was forty-nine, and at that age had settled himself into a slot as Van Houten's promotional man, which meant he had the problem of making all the stars at the studio book good. His number one problem was Holly Hill. His ruddy pock-marked complexion grinned up at Dan. He brushed back a lock of sandy red hair.

"I heard that Holly was after you," he laughed, grinning even more broadly.

"Hell, damned, and hell again. If that's what you wanted to see me about, you came at the right time. I just got the word from the Big Boy!"

"No, as a matter of fact, no. It's about Doris Patton." His face grew serious.

"What about Doris?" Dan asked, stepping into the *Shack-Off,* a restaurant, and saloon. They made their way into a corner booth, ordered two double Scotches, and then settled back.

"Well," Dan asked, "What about Doris?"

"Well, I don't know where to start, really," Elliott said, studying his freckled thick fingers which were nervously playing against one another.

"Start at the beginning. I didn't know you two where running together."

"We aren't. Only that...hell, to be truthful...the other day, it hit me. I saw her walking across the studio lot, and suddenly it hit me—and...to be honest, Dan, I'd give one hell of a lot to date the woman."

Dan frowned. "Why tell me about it?"

Elliott shrugged. The drinks came then and it wasn't until they had taken their first swallows that Elliott said anything else.

"I heard you two were making the point...and, well, I didn't want to walk on your toes...

"Hell, that was months ago. Anyway, it was only a casual thing." Dan took another swallow of his Scotch, lighted a cigarette and dragged several puffs before the other said anything.

"Hell, Dan, to be truthful, I don't know how to go about it." Elliott looked embarrassed.

"You kidding—the old sex writer, shy?" Dan couldn't believe it. "You—afraid of a woman? I've seen you running, chasing, and playing with a hundred. What makes Doris different?"

They finished off their drinks before Elliott answered.

"I think I could really go for Doris, Dan...it just hit me like that—and it gutted out all my guts at the same time. She's so damned—hell, I'm just some slob with personality—Sam-bam bursting out all over. She hardly notices me. Anyway, it's different from chasing...and, to be truthful, what kind of gal is she?"

"That's not a nice question, Elliott—"

"Oh, come on, Dan—I didn't mean what kind of lay...well, lover she is...I meant...do you think I'd be wasting my time—you know, trying the serious thing with her?" He gulped on his second Scotch.

"Hell, Elliott, I'm not her father-confessor. Who knows what kind of woman any girl is...in any case, you don't know if you really would go for her—personally—in the first place. You surprise me..." His voice faded off. Elliott was nervously lighting a cigarette and not quite making it.

"Look, Dan, I'm old enough to know what I'm doing. I've knocked around long enough—I'm tired of the old chasing game—ready to settle down—and...well, I've seen Doris around—just never realized how I felt about her...I've thought a lot about this, Dan—I never made a pass at Doris—and it wasn't because I didn't want to. It just struck me why...and knowing why, I could do it now—but I'd

49

be serious about the thing. What's she like?"

"A good secretary—a nice girl. She's been around enough to know it takes more than bed sleeping to get into movies. I don't think she's interested in a career. Is that what you mean?"

"Partly. Maybe that's all you can tell me." Elliott was silent, and had finished his cigarette by the time he said anything else.

"Thanks, Dan...I guess I sound like a damned fool. Only thing—I didn't want to stick out my neck too far...not *that* way. A guy gets knocked around and hurt enough not to want any more hurts. I fell some years back—and got my head knocked off. She wanted a career—so that was it." He hesitated and then said: "That was Holly."

Dan tried to say something but didn't know the words. Finally he merely said: "I'm sorry."

"Hell, what's there to be sorry about? That was years ago…too many—when she was just a starlet. It's over now—for a long, long time. Ancient history. I was just young enough and foolish enough to think...well, maybe it was just that she...hell, that was my first love affair—I don't mind admitting it now. She was only eighteen...I was twenty-nine— see...twenty years ago...hell, twenty years ago—I don't mind admitting it—I'm getting up in years— about time I thought about settling down. So...it's over with, now." He looked seriously at Dan. "Do me a favor, Dan."

The voice was so serious that Dan snapped his eyes up, probed into Elliott's. "What?"

"Be nice to her...she's had it...I mean some real hard ones—try to be nice to her...just for me?"

"You still soft on Holly?"

"Hell...of course. Isn't a guy always soft on his first love? Even if he's over it?" Elliott laughed. "Hell—let's get back to the office so I can try making time with that secretary of yours."

Dan nodded, finished off his drink and tried not to think about that evening with Holly Hill.

Holly Hill, the dream of every red-blooded American. He was lucky.

To hell he was lucky!

Once back in the office, Dan had Doris get Holly Hill on the phone.

"Holly, Dan Blair."

Holly's voice was harsh through the receiver. "You...decide you aren't so high and mighty powerful and—"

"Holly, honey, simmer down and give a guy a break," he soothed, as warmly as he could. "I'm only human!"

"So?"

There was a long silence while Dan tried to find the words. Finally he decided on the direct approach.

"About the other night...I never dreamed you were really serious. Hell, Holly...I've never been quite so flattered. What man wouldn't be flattered when Holly Hill shows interest? Damned if I'm not still shaking from the reaction. When Murry said you'd been serious...Holly, believe me, even if you were some nobody...a guy like me would consider himself damned lucky to have your interest. He'd crawl on his hands and knees, begging for a date! You have to understand that I was slightly drunk— and...I didn't have any idea that you could really be actually making a pass at me and—"

"Cut it out, lover," she demanded coldly. "Just give it to me straight."

"That's the straight dope, Holly."

There was a long, loud silence after that. He could hear her breathing on the other end of the line. Sweat was trickling down his forehead; a grinding sensation was churning at the pit of his stomach.

Finally she said: "Why don't you come over here, tonight. I don't have anything important planned…and maybe we could have a little party all our own. Now that would be kinda nice, don't you think?"

He was quick to say: "I was hoping you'd understand and ask me over."

"At seven—no...make it eight-thirty sharp, darling. I don't like to be kept waiting!"

"Fine."

"I'm glad you called, darling," she murmured in her most sexy screen voice. "I was beginning to believe you'd been...well, let's forget about all that. I'll be looking forward to our meeting…and don't be shy! I'm not at all shy, you'll soon discover!"

Dan was still sweating as he hung the receiver on the hook. It was going to be one hell of a long evening; longer than any he had lived through for a long time. He'd heard about Holly Hill's way of making love, and the invitation of her sexy body was only over-shadowed by the vivid stories he had heard about this queen of Van Houten Studios.

CHAPTER FIVE

Dan sat in his car, parked outside the huge house where Holly Hill lived. It was expensive as only a Beverly Hills home could be. The lawn stretched out in front like an expanse of dark green velvet. Two large trees commanded the lawn like huge shadowy guards, standing there, to protect Holly Hill, Queen of Van Houten Studios.

Dan put out his third cigarette. Looking at his watch, he sighed and then lighted another cigarette, got out of the car and started across the lonely street toward the monstrous estate.

Holly had said she would expect him at eight-thirty. It was eight-twenty nine. If he was one second late the earth would shake, the sky fall, and "Chicken Little" would be running around jobless, begging for hand-outs.

He laughed silently at himself, remembering the thoughts which had plagued him in the morning.

Who would it be this night? That Gale something-or-other? No! It wouldn't be Gale Ross; or anybody else except the Queen.

"Well," he muttered to himself, "You'll find out if that blonde hair is real or bleached!"

Standing in the small alcove of the darkened

porch, Dan felt the grind at the pit of his stomach.

Was it worth it? Hell, what was wrong with him? Holly Hill and her big boobs—every man in the world wanted Holly Hill; to find the holly in her hills

He laughed, half drunkenly. The cocktails had gotten to him.

He wished he were with a Gale Ross.

Dan hesitated before ringing the doorbell. He thought about the young, tall blonde who had been in his office that afternoon. Gale Ross: what a beautiful woman. What a fiery temper. It had surprised Dan when she'd burst out at him. What a delightful temper.

And what a reaction the one physical contact had made. Then he forgot about Gale Ross and pressed the button.

Dan stood there, waiting. And waiting. It seemed too long.

The door swung open suddenly and a tall, stuffy looking old man stood there.

"Mr. Blair, nice to see you, sir."

Dan nodded and walked in. "Where's Holly?"

"In the drawing room, sir," the butler said, closing the door and disappearing.

Taking a deep breath, Dan walked across the entranceway and into a large, expensively furnished living room. A huge fireplace centered across from the entrance, with a large oil painting of Holly Hill hanging over it.

The sound of music came from a speaker, behind the bamboo bar. The lighting was just staged right: low but not dim. Shadows played over the room, flickering from the fire in the marble fireplace.

Dan tried to find Holly, but it didn't seem as if she were there. A large green sofa centered in the middle of the room, in front of the fire place. A thin trail of smoke weaved its way up from behind it.

"Hello, Darling," Holly's voice sounded from the sofa.

"So, there you are...Holly," Dan greeted, trying to make his voice sound interested.

She popped up.

A low cut, tight fitting cream colored sweater hugged her large breasts. Her arms were covered with bracelets. A long cigarette holder extended from her right hand. She looked at him, her plush lips half parted, her large, brown-green eyes veiled impersonally. "Well, it's about time you showed up."

"I'm here—on the dot!" Dan countered, making a big display of looking at his watch.

"Darling, you should know a woman likes her men early." Her eyes flared at him. "You're a bastard, Mister Blair."

"Now, what'd I do?" He tried to look innocent.

"Nothing—that's what. That...tramp you were with. She spread her quivering thighs for you?" Her voice was high and nastily sharp.

"Oh, that...look, Holly, I must have been out of my mind—hell, who would—"

"Cut the crap, Darling and mix yourself a drink!" Her eyes moved to the bar.

"Want one?" he asked.

"Have one."

She disappeared behind the sofa.

Dan moved to the bar; walked around it and

looked at the healthy liquor supply. He picked out a bottle of Scotch dropped two ice cubes into a glass and poured himself a stiff drink.

"Darling, come on over, I want to see you!" Holly demanded in a tight voice.

Dan stepped to the sofa, looked down at Holly.

She was stretched out, her eyes meeting his, evenly. A tight-fitting skirt showed off her voluptuous figure. For a woman her age, Holly had kept her figure better than most girls a dozen years younger. Maybe her breasts were softening up a little. Hard to tell. Maybe her hips were getting a light covering of bulge, but she looked as sexy as on the screen— maybe more so. It was only her face that age showed. Lines which didn't show on film crinkled around her brown-green eyes. Her lips were a little too generous, but sensual enough to be quite undesirable.

"Like what you see, Darling?" Holly asked in her most sultry voice.

"Why not?"

"That's not an answer." Her eyes narrowed slightly, her lips compressed into hardness.

"You're the image of beauty!" He took a deep swallow of his drink, and found himself thinking about Gale Ross. *Now, why should he be thinking about that spitfire?*

"I'm glad you came over, Darling," Holly was saying. "After the other night I didn't think you had anything for me...I mean...I thought maybe you dug men or something."

He stared at her. She was mocking him with her eyes.

"To be truthful," he said in his most diplomatic

56

voice, "I didn't believe you even knew I existed."

"What in the world made you think that, Darling?" she pouted, reaching up and touching his arm. "You got any muscles?"

Reluctantly he tightened his arm and she murmured in pleasure at the hardness her fingers caressed.

"I thought you'd look good in a bathing suit!" She laughed, popped up to a sitting position. Her legs hugged against the swell of her breasts. "How about it?"

"What?"

"A swim? Naked!" She laughed, letting her eyes run over his body, hungrily devouring him.

"Darling, I don't know if I could stand taking a naked swim with you—but I want to try!" She laughed again and stood, pressed herself against him, and rolled her hips in rhythm with the music sounding in the background. She felt his reaction and made a surprised face. "You really are a man, aren't you, Darling?"

Holly stepped away and moved to the bar, swinging her large hips from side to side.

Dan realized that everything about Holly was large. She was one hell of a bitching woman; that much he could give her.

Why did she demanded lovers the way she'd done with him? It didn't make sense. He shrugged down the thought and took another swallow of his drink.

As Holly mixed herself a Martini, her eyes kept lashing out at him, burning from excitement to anger.

"I should hate you, Darling," she said in a biting, sharp voice. "Nobody ever turned me down like that!"

"I didn't turn you down, Holly. I didn't know what I was doing—and even if I had—I couldn't very well let that girl…"

"That girl is a bitch—and she's finished at the studio!" Holly snapped, gulping down the Martini.

"What! You didn't—"

"Get her fired? Why not?" She shrugged and her breasts danced in the sweater. It was the first time that Dan realized she was braless. He wondered if there was anything on under her skirt. He doubted it.

"How about our swim, Darling," she suggested in a tone which was more a challenge than anything else. She walked up to him, took his arm and pulled him out of the room.

There was nothing subtle about Holly. She knew what she wanted and wasn't about to play silly social games. And, in fact, her first comment supported that, as they left the room.

"I don't see why we should be coy. We know why you're here. We know what I want. So, I hope you don't mind my not doing a big conversational scene to build up some kind of seductive mood. I've acted that out too many times in the movies. Rather boring, if you want to know the truth. If a girl wants to be fucked she should say so. Don't you think? Well, I'm not shy about my desires. And there's no stupid script writer to feed me lines. I do quite well, all by myself. So…let's strip and admire one another before getting down to basics!"

They walked across the house and then out onto the patio, then to the immense swimming pool. They stood at the edge for a short while, silently

58

staring into the cool green depths.

"Water is so sensual, flowing around your naked skin. Caressing every nerve. I enjoy swimming in the raw. Don't you?"

He merely shrugged.

"You haven't done that."

"Didn't say."

"You haven't!" she laughed. "Well, I suppose I'll be something of a new experience for you, Darling!"

Dan felt like a male prostitute; and disgusted at what was happening. How could a woman play this kind of game? Surely she realized the truth; realized that he was only there because she'd demanded it. Or didn't it matter to her. Maybe her game was enjoying outright power over men. If that was so, she had proven her point with him. Why the illusion of sexual intimacy? What made her demand having his body?

"You know, Darling, I was thrilled you wanted to see me. A girl likes to be wanted. And I know you want me. Most men do. Rather natural, don't you think, Darling? After all, I'm studio promoted as the hottest thing in the universe! Something to really live up to. I hope you aren't disappointed. Well, I doubt you will be. My men enjoy me fully. I love a good, strong man. A big male with hard muscles all over his body. And you sure have a hard one! I could feel that! And I'll make you love me so good! I'm going to make you enjoy every inch of me, every delicious moment! I can promise you that much!" She sat down at the edge of the pool, put her legs in the water, shivering, laughing. Then she lifted her skirt high over her legs, into a circle around a narrowed waist. As he'd guessed, she didn't have anything on underneath; and she was a natural blonde.

"Like what you see?" she inquired, not even glancing his way at that point. "Most men find my body a real charge. I work hard to keep it in top shape!"

With a quick action, she pulled the sweater over her head. Her eyes, now, turned to meet his. Holly reached up for Dan, urged him down beside her. She pressed his hand against one large fleshy breast.

He was surprised to discover how firm she felt. Probably a little softer than when Elliott had been known her, but still youthful! In fact, amazingly more youthful than they deserved to be at her age. She played his hand over her breast.

"You're going to be fun!" she laughed, suddenly dropping his hand, standing and unzipping her skirt. She kicked the skirt back, away from her feet and challenged him with her eyes. "Come on, Darling—off with the garments!"

With that, Holly dived into the pool, the impact of her large body splashed his clothing.

Standing, Dan finished off his drink, set the glass down on the pool-side, and slowly started undressing.

Holly came up for air, turned, looked at him and shouted: "Hurry, Darling—I can't wait!"

Dirty bitch! he said to himself, feeling a sense of satisfaction of having actually thought it.

"Okay—keep your panties on!"

"I don't have them on! Surely you must have noticed I'm all beautifully naked down there, and it's just waiting..." she laughed, diving under the water. Then she surfaced, grinning in delight at him. Her eyes were literally stroking his whole frame. She watched for a long moment, then submerged under the water.

As he pulled off the last piece of his clothing, Holly surfaced again, right in front of him. She grabbed his ankle, almost pulling him off balance. With a curse, Dan fell into the pool, close to her.

As he swam across the pool, he was aware of the woman swimming beside him, but tried to ignore her. The water was cool, but not cold. The shock of it had numbed away the booze effect and he felt almost sober. When he had reached the far side, Holly was right next to him. She reached out, and suddenly they were pressing close, her large mouth covering his, her body doing an impassioned twist.

Holly laughed, and teased his back with her long sharp fingernails.

"Damn it!" he cursed, attempting to shove her away.

"What's wrong, Darling, don't you like a hot passionate woman?" She teased him again with her fingers, daring him with her eyes, laughing all the time.

Her eyes closed, her lips hung open, and her tongue darted out, touching his mouth.

His whole body responded to her nearness. She was overwhelming.

Dan caressed her fanny and she trembled against him, her breasts cushioned moistly against his slippery wet flesh.

He felt her mouth close over his shoulder.

She moaned as if in ecstasy, her eyes half

closed, the pupils disappeared upwards, her lips trembled wide open. A throaty sound uttered from her chest. Then Holly pressed even closer.

"Now, Darling...now...I...can't...wait! Please don't let me wait!"

Startled, Dan tried to tell the woman how impossible it was in the pool, but as her voluptuous body moved sensually against his, he realized that it was possible, that in fact it was already happening.

They were waist high in the water when their bodies blended. She tensed, as if afraid he would disappear. Racking sobs choked her throat. Heaving gasps were pounding her breasts up and down against his chest.

Then, just as the ecstasy was beginning to blind its way over his vision, beginning to surge erotic needles over every nerve, Dan fell over backwards. He felt the woman twist away. He was sure she would blame him for frustrating her. He'd never hear the last of it. As he struggled to his feet, shaking the water from his face, Dan saw Holly standing there, an excited broad grin on her face.

"Darling—you're *wonderful!*" She hugged him, and then slipped away. "Beat you to the other end. Then bedsville—real fun and games!"

Holly started across the pool. She swam fast; much faster than he would have thought possible. Dan followed, slower.

As he swam toward the other end of the pool, Dan found himself wondering about Holly Hill. He thought about Elliott Wood; a man who had always seemed the personality-Sam, who had once been in love with this sex-pot. *Be nice to her*, Elliott had made him promise. He'd started out pretty damned

62

good. What kind of woman *was* Holly Hill? A love-hungry woman approaching middle age. Desperately afraid of growing old, but still magnificently attractive.

Climbing out of the pool behind Holly, he followed her into the large house. They both walked through the expensively carpeted rooms, dripping wet, completely naked, down the hall, up the stairs. Neither said a word.

They walked into a large room with frilly decorations. A huge, king-sized bed centered the room, the covers drawn back, ready, waiting.

Everything was seductive about Holly and she was making no excuses, and making no effort to hide her desires for the evening.

She stopped in front of the bed, turned and grinned at him.

"Come on, Darling, this is what I've been waiting for—the main event!" Her arms reached out for him.

Christ, he thought, she hadn't even offered a build up. He'd arrived, followed by a short conversational exchange, and then into the pool and now this.

Dan tried to grin, almost afraid to take up the commanding offer. After the little performance at the pool, he could wait a life-time before learning what she considered the main event.

She stood there like a sensual Goddess of Love. Her arms flung out as she offered her greatest gift. Her large, supple breasts presented themselves like tempting beacons to drive a man to his bloody death on the rocks that lay in some invisible void. It was an invitation no man could possibly ignore or escape. Invitation to doom in the arms of the Voluptuous Goddess of Ecstasy.

What more could any man ask? What more could any American—or any male animal the world over—ask? Holly Hill, the queen of the movies—Holly Hill, sensual offering, dished out to the public like cigarettes. Holly Hill, middle-aged sex symbol, hungry for love, hungry to know that she was still desired by every man in the world. Holly Hill, a world of sensual pleasures, spread out like a banquet to taste, to feast, to devour.

He walked to her, feeling a sinking nausea gulp his insides, knowing that what all men desired held a price-tag. Dan could feel some of the marking of her price-tag scraped on his back and chest, stinging, burning. She was a hellion she-cat, and making love to Holly Hill was like making love to a lioness in heat.

Holly folded her arms around him and fell backwards against the softness of the thick mattress, laughing, her lips finally covering his lips, her body writhing, twisting, her finger-nails tensing for attack.

After the first few wild moments he wasn't thinking, he was moving, feeling, and actually finding enjoyment.

During those wild moments when she folded around him like hot velvet, he even forgot it was Holly Hill; the woman who had commanded his body for the night. He even forgot that he was the male-prostitute making love to her like he'd never loved a woman before, in order to keep his job.

Only after they had tired of each other; only after Holly had fallen exhausted on the bed, did Dan wonder how long this would have to continue. How many days and nights would her hunger for him continue to demand feeding? How many weeks would she want him to come to this bedroom?

The only way he could find escape from his troubled thoughts was by thinking about that young blonde who had come into the office and spit fire at him, first verbally and then physically in that one impulsive contact. He wondered why he enjoyed thinking about her.

Only after he'd decided to arrange a date with Gale could he find rest. It was a strangely perverse realization: he wanted to see the woman, very much so. Something about the woman had fascinated him almost instantly. The verbal fire between them might be nothing more than a cover-up for mutual desire.

Some time in the middle of the night Holly called to him and he could do nothing other than answer the call.

His whole career depended upon it.

In the morning, Holly announced, "Darling, we gotta make a habit of this." She kissed him on the lips. "Gotta make a habit of it." Then she leaned over, pressed her breast against his mouth. "How about a morning pick-up?" she inquired. "I just love the way you kiss them. So kiss 'em, Darlin'."

There wasn't any way to escape. He gave her a pick-up he didn't know existed in him. Afterwards, he thanked God she was happy to let him get dressed and leave with a promise to call in the afternoon.

CHAPTER SIX

Gale had let Mildred make love to her the night before. She thrilled to the woman's body and her lush, greedy love-making. Yet, afterwards she could only think about the excitement of Dan Blair's touch.

That afternoon, before going to work, Gale called Dan Blair's office, and left her phone number.

At work, Loreen Asher, another cocktail waitress trying to get into the movies, trapped Gale in the kitchen.

Loreen was a thin girl, but attractive enough to get constant attention from the men. She had dark blonde hair, which was too natural, and a nasal sounding voice that killed her chances as a movie actress; but she didn't admit that.

"What happened with your interview?" Loreen wanted to know. The girl had been off the night before and hadn't had a chance to question Gale.

"A Mr. Dan Blair gave me a part in some television production," Gale said, feeling awkward at putting on a show for Loreen. But the girl was so young, so inexperienced in the ways of Hollywood, and Gale had knocked around so long, that is felt good to be able to brag.

"What kind of guy is he?"

"Terribly good looking," Gale said, happily.

"Did he make a pass at you? Did you have to sleep with him?" Loreen asked, whispering the question so that nobody else could hear.

"Of course not!"

"Will you have to?"

"Why?"

"I thought girls always had to sleep their way up. I wouldn't mind," she admitted frankly.

Gale laughed to herself. No doubt about that, she thought. Loreen Asher was almost a joke around the restaurant. She picked up with a different guy every night. *Swinging Loreen*, they called her.

"Would you sleep with him?" Loreen wanted to know, her eyes all eager, all wide innocence.

Gale hesitated, wanting to put the woman in her place, but then realized that Loreen just didn't understand that such subjects should be personal.

"That hasn't come up—and I don't think it will." That ended the subject and Gale went back to serving the customers at the bar.

After work, Gale had a couple of cocktails and then drove home. Mildred was in bed, but awake.

"Hello, honey," Mildred said, as Gale slipped under the covers.

The woman moved close, her thigh touching Gale's.

"I was waiting up," Mildred said.

It was the secret message that meant Mildred wanted to make love to Gale.

Mildred pressed delicate fingers into Gale's breast, then slipped them under the top of her pajamas, tickled across a soft supple breast.

Gale thrilled to the caress. A wave of desire suddenly burst alive in her.

"I need it, Gale...I need it..." Mildred moaned in a hungry voice. She turned and pressed her hefty breasts against Gale's side. "Please...Gale."

Without a word Gale embraced the woman, let the kisses search over her lips. But it was the thrilling shock of Dan Blair's touch that drove her mind and deed.

"I love you, Gale," Mildred murmured, "Love you so much...."

The voice trailed out of reality as the sensual world slashed over every thought, every nerve. Gale lay back, bathing in Mildred's soft, yielding flesh.

And then she found herself thinking about Dan Blair, and wondering what it might be like in his arms.

It had been so long, so very long since she had experienced love with a man. It was impossible for Gale to remember what it was like.

"I love you, Gale," Mildred breathed in her ear. "I don't want to lose you...ever!"

The words of love unnerved Gale. She didn't want Mildred to be in love with her. That was the last thing she ever wanted. In fact the relationship was beginning to make her feel uneasy. Strangely enough she could still response to Mildred's lovemaking. But, then, the woman was skilled.

And I'm needy! Gale realized.

She felt the other woman slip closer, gently place an arm around her. It was in the intimate closeness of Mildred's body that Gale found relaxation from her thoughts. At least she wasn't alone.

Her last thought was merely how long could this affair last—that she needed much more in life than what Mildred could give. One hell of a lot more.

This affair, if that's what it should be called, had to end, before it was too late.

Maybe it was already too late to avoid a nasty scene.

CHAPTER SEVEN

A couple of days had passed since Elliott Wood had talked to Dan about Doris Patton. Two days of hectic production problems. The advertisement company was on Dan's neck to push production of the pilot. He was having troubles casting a couple of the supporting roles, and Holly Hill had been pressing all his free time into love-sessions that left his nerves and body shattered in the morning. He was drinking too much and coming to work jagged. He was smoking one cigarette after another.

It was mid-morning when Elliott came into his office, slamming down some copy for the show Dan was casting. After the normal conversational niceties, Elliott leaned back in his chair and asked: "What you have planned for the weekend?"

Dan gave the man a nasty look. "Nothing—but..."

"But Holly has plans for you?" Elliott inquired with a grin. "How you two getting along?"

"You said be nice to her—hell, man, why didn't you call her up and tell her to be nice to me?"

Elliott frowned, lighted a cigarette and then asked:

"What's wrong?"

"Now, come on, buddy, don't give me that!"

The expression on Elliott's face convinced Dan that the man had no idea what he was talking about. A worried expression clouded his face. "Didn't Holly play—?"

"She's as wild as they come, Elliott..." Dan groaned, then tried to force a grin. "As for the weekend...I could use a vacation—*from* Holly!"

"Why not? I'm planning a stint at Las Vegas—with your lovely secretary," Elliott grinned.

"Coming along?"

"Of course. Beautifully!" The man's face grew serious again. "How about it?"

"With Holly?" Dan countered, uneasily.

"Hell, no! Maybe Helen Biggs...or any other young thing that looks like fun," Elliott suggested. "You could certainly find some excuse to beg off with Holly. Tell a little white lie—say you're sick, or something. Just a couple of days, fun in the sun... how about it?"

Dan shrugged and promised to think about it. He didn't until later that afternoon when Doris handed him a memo with Gale Ross's name, address, phone number and work number on it. It was in line with the part that had been okayed for the woman. He stared at the name, for a moment forgetting who Gale was, then he remembered and picked up the phone, dialed.

A feminine voice answered with a throaty hello.

"Is Gale there?"

"Yes, just a moment."

Silence, then, "Hello?"

"This is Dan Blair, at Van Houten Studios—about that part you interviewed for—we want you on the set, Monday morning."

"Oh, great, what time?"

"Well, we could talk over the details...well, to tell the truth, Gale—I can call you that?"

"Of course."

Impulsively, without thinking, he blurted: "Well, I called...wondering if you'd like to take a trip to Las Vegas over the weekend and—"

"Is that *necessary?*" she demanded, icily.

He hesitated, then said: "No—has nothing to do with the part—only I thought maybe that—"

"I don't think so, Mister Blair. I'm not about to...well, just play around...especially when it's not necessary...I hardly know you!" She paused, then quickly put in, "Maybe some other time—once we've gotten to know each other?" Her voice was inviting, but formal. "But certainly you can under-stand...we don't even know one another!"

"Well, can't blame a man for trying."

"Hardly flattering."

"I didn't mean to insult you," he retorted, want-ing to kick himself for having blunder so badly. "I really do want to know you better. Is there anything wrong with that?"

She hesitated for a moment then said: "I sup-pose not. But..."

"But nothing. Come on, give a guy a break!"

"Why?"

"Because I'm a nice guy?"

"Nice guys don't make such brazenly crude of-fers to a woman they have never even dated be-fore!" She sounded icy, again.

Dan shrugged to himself, said "Well, it was an idea." After a few short sentences, he brought the conversation to an end. He had blundered terribly with the woman. A very stupid move. With some of the girls that run through his office such a suggestive invitation might have been accepted. He had been stupid to make it with Gale.

Putting the receiver on the hook, Dan studied the slip of paper with Gale's numbers, then crumpled it up. About to throw it in the waste basket, Dan changed his mind and pocketed it instead. He forgot all about it until later that evening while sitting alone in a cocktail lounge. This was the first evening that Holly had been busy with some studio director—his first "night off." He remembered the slip of paper in his pocket. He looked at it and saw a work number listed. Below the number was the name of a restaurant: *Chambers Steak House. Call after six in the evening.* He considered and made a snap decision.

Maybe after a little personal contact, she might reconsider about the weekend in Las Vegas, all expenses paid. Or at the very least, maybe he could sooth over the error he'd made and begin fresh. And who knew where that might lead. At least he wouldn't be totally alone this evening. And the idea of seeing Gale again was actually quite inviting, even exciting.

Without even being aware of having done so, he drove to the *Chambers Steak House.*

The restaurant was one of those flashy places with thick red carpets, oak-wood decorations, dim lighting. He asked the head waiter about Gale Ross, learned she worked in the cocktail lounge and made his way into the long, narrow room that sported fifteenth-century armor. He settled into a booth and waited for a waitress to come for his order.

There was a piano bar in the center of the room. A musician was tinkling out a Latin rhythm, surrounded by a flock of half-drunk customers.

A tall, thin cocktail waitress in a low cut evening gown gave him a view of her supple looking breasts as she bent over the table to place a cocktail napkin in front of him. The view was inviting. It was meant to be seductive—of a tip later. She smiled, warmly.

"What can I do for you?" she asked.

"Give me a double Martini, and tell Gale Ross that Mr. Blair is here to see her."

"Gale's not working tonight...but she'll be here tomorrow and—say, aren't you the producer of something?" Her face lighted up, showing even more seductive invitation.

"Dan Blair at your service. How about the Martini, sweetie," he said. Dan watched the woman slink across the room to put in his order. She stood by the waitress station, looking at him, her eyes playing anxiously with his. Obviously she was more than interested in being picked up.

Dan considered. He could call Gale at her home, but that wouldn't get him very far. Here was a young thing just eager to spend a night with somebody like him. She hadn't been too subtle. He studied her too slender figure, hesitated and decided it wasn't the package as much as the action—what she did that counted. He didn't have anything better to do; and the drinks had warmed a sensual glow over his body. The idea of spending a night with some girl, other than Holly Hill, was suddenly appealing.

When the woman came back to his table, he

74

asked:

"What's your name, sweetie?"

"Loreen…Asher."

"You're sure one lovely lady."

"Well, thank you. I noticed you right off. A real looker, if you ask me."

"Should I ask you?" he grinned.

"What?" she quickly inquired, then swiftly offered: "Ask me any thing you like. I'm an open book." And her eyes said he could read each and every page just for the asking.

Without any doubt as to her response, he asked: "Doing anything after work?"

She grinned and shook her head. "But I'm open for suggestions."

"Suggestion given. We might find some intimate place to talk it over," he offered, grinning back.

"Conversation or conversation is my motto!" she grinned. "Verbal or otherwise."

"You sound like one hell of a cooperative young woman."

"I'm more than cooperative," she admitted without hesitation. "I'm an actress, too."

"No way!" he exclaimed, not at all surprised.

"Of course. This is just a temp job. I'm really into the Hollywood scene."

"Been in any films?"

"Well, in some plays, if you know what I mean. I'm…willing to do anything to get ahead in the business. I know how important contacts can be."

"Well, I never make promises I can't keep," he chuckled. "But I'd sure like to give you a personal, private interview tonight."

"Real personal and very private?" she inquired with a knowing smile. "I kinda like that idea. I'm off at one...you still be here?"

"It's about ten-thirty...maybe. I'll meet you, in any case."

As it turned out he was still there, after three double Martinis, slightly drunk and not caring about anything much in the world other than the playing around with Loreen Asher.

When she had finished work, he escorted her to his car. Twenty minutes later they were stepping into his apartment.

"What a set-up...but a big producer like you must have plenty of money," Loreen said breathlessly.

He started to correct her about his position and then decided to play along with the game. "Well, Lorrie, we get a little cash now and then to spend."

She glided to the home bar in the corner as he turned on the lights which bathed the large room in romantic blue.

After mixing drinks, he led Loreen into the bedroom, closed the door and sat on the bed. She didn't hesitate to sit down beside him.

"I've never been with a producer before," Loreen announced in an enthralled voice. She looked up into his eyes, her face lighted with excitement. "It's really a thrill, Mr. Blair."

"Dan."

"You're nice...Dan," she cooed, leaning close, so he could look down her neckline. "I like you. Liked you from the first minute I walked up to the table to take your order."

"I wonder if you've been in a man's apartment,

76

at all," he accused her, teasingly.

Loreen laughed.

"Okay, so you're been around."

"You bet your sweet life, Dan. I've been around enough to make you really like me," she announced in a husky voice. "You won't be sorry you invited me."

Dan shrugged, downed his drink and put the glass on the floor.

She came into his arms without a word, her lips open wide. She tensed as they rolled back onto the bed; Dan suddenly found pleasure in what was happening. So different from Holly Hill. At least it was better than being alone, wanting to be with Gale.

Later, much later, he learned all there was to know about Loreen Asher. He discovered the tiny mole on her left breast, the other, larger one which hid on her thigh. And he learned all the buttons to press to make her motor race. Afterwards he knew there wasn't anything more to discover and was glad when they fell asleep.

She was gone when he awoke in the morning. He didn't even question how she'd gotten home, or when she had left. It was enough to be rid of her. He needed a woman that could reach deeper than a one-night stand, who could touch an emotional chord within him. He thought of Gale Ross, and once more wondered why he even bothered thinking about her. They didn't even know one another!

Another day faced him, and another night with Holly Hill. He wondered why he hadn't spent his night off to rest up after her explosive, demanding lust-making. Maybe he'd looked for something that didn't exist, some haven that would give him escape.

Dan needed a drink to face the long day. He ended up in having two drinks, and was a little high as he drove to the office.

CHAPTER EIGHT

Gale listened to the prattling of Loreen as she related the long detailed tale of how she had managed to set herself up for a night of excitement and pleasure with a Dan Blair.

"Then I slipped out, real mysterious...he'll be going crazy wondering...thinking I didn't like his love-making. That's how to get a man interested," Loreen announced, sure of herself, her eyes gleaming in victory. "Gosh, he's the damndest! A real swinger!"

That was something from Loreen.

Gale went through the rest of the night, dazed, hating that fact that it had been necessary to turn Dan Blair down for the weekend. But they didn't even know one another. And she wasn't like Loreen. It had been the casual, so-sure-of-himself way in which he'd asked her, as if she'd fly out of her panties in eagerness to have a weekend in Las Vegas with him.

Maybe she'd made a mistake turning him down. On the other hand, it would have been impossible. Under the right circumstances, that might be something else. If they dated and discovered they actually liked one another; well, then she would surely con-

79

sider such an invitation as at least somewhat inviting, rather than insulting. But maybe he was actually interested in her.

After all, she told herself, annoyed, he'd come to her place of work, just to look her up.

That was somewhat thrilling. She would like to know him better.

That night she slept restlessly, dreaming, but not remembering what the dreams were all about. The next morning she found herself pacing the apartment, nervously. Several times she stopped at the phone, tempted to call Dan Blair and say she had reconsidered his offer. But the idea was impossible. She couldn't call a man up and say she'd changed her mind; that just wasn't done. Plus she wasn't some kind of slut on the make.

She fixed herself a drink, stared at it for a long time, then sipped, then gulped.

Gale found herself standing by the phone, trying to find the phrases that would sound logical to tell Dan Blair that she wanted to go to Vegas with him. Arms distant and all that, but the two of them in separate rooms, of course, and everything respectable.

Hello, Mr. Blair, would you mind terribly, but I decided that after what happened the other night...I would like to reconsidered, and accept!

You know, a girl has a right to change her mind. How about asking me again?

She picked up the receiver and then dropped it back on the hook. She mixed herself another drink. Sipped, gulped.

For a dizzy moment the room spun and then righted itself. She was holding the receiver to her ear.

A voice was saying.

"Van Houten Studios."

She was saying: "Could I speak to Dan Blair?"

"Who is calling, please?"

"Tell him Miss Ross."

Doris Patton: "Mr. Blair's office."

"This is Gale Ross, is Mr. Blair in?"

Gale was shaking as she waited for the secretary to answer.

"Yes, just a moment, I'll connect you."

She waited, holding her breath, suddenly wondering what she would say, and for a moment almost hanging up the phone.

Then a mannish voice said: "Hello, Miss Ross?"

It was too late to turn back now, she had plunged and now she either sank or swam.

* * * * * * *

Dan felt a strange reaction at hearing Gale Ross's voice. But he didn't have time to puzzle over the matter.

She was saying:

"I just wanted to call...tell you how sorry I was about the other day—it wasn't very nice of me, considering how nice you were to ask me to...well, I felt like a terrible fool, and I hoped you would understand, if I called and told you how I felt about it. You know, Mr. Blair...well, I know this will sound silly, but...I've thought a lot about you—I mean, since leaving your office that day...and, I know that we could really have a lot of fun together, if only given the chance. It would be nice...getting to know each other. I suppose. I don't know what was wrong with me the other day, so silly, you know..."

Her voice was nervous sounding, the words running faster and faster together.

And on and on, rattling, slightly slurred words, meaningless words which merely blended into a flow of pleasant sounds he sat there listening to.

She has a nice sounding voice, Dan thought, smiling at the receiver. *A very nice, pleasant voice.*

But from the tone, the slight slur, Dan couldn't help thinking that this Gale Ross wasn't the kind of woman that took herself so casually. From the blur of words, one would have thought she was throwing herself at him—and possibly every man who came along. But he couldn't believe that. Maybe she was foolish enough to believe that by letting him have his way with her body he'd help her career along. Yet that hadn't seemed reasonable, considering Van Houten had put the pressure on. He wondered just how well Van Houten knew Gale.

"Miss Ross," Dan finally broke in, realizing how long he had been listening to her voice. "It's all right—I understand."

A long silence. Then a word question: "Well?"

"Well, what?" he countered.

"Well, well...what do you think?" she blurted out over the receiver, her voice harsh, edged sharp.

"I'll call you up some time next week—maybe for dinner and cocktails—if that's what you mean," Dan told her, hoping it would give her the hint. The weekend thing was off, as far as this Gale Ross was concerned, and if she'd called to change her mind, it was too late. He'd already asked Helen, Murry Van Houten's secretary.

A short silence and then: "Well, I'd be delighted!"

Dan hurriedly said good-bye and hung up the phone. He sat there thinking about Gale Ross for a few moments and then the thoughts slipped from his mind. There were other things needing his attention; and they had nothing to do with any Gale Ross; or with any female companionship—at all!

CHAPTER NINE

They were staying at the Sands, the flashy Las Vegas club that featured a group of big named stars which had once been known to the public as the Clan.

Dan sat at the roulette table spreading dollar chips across the board. The little white ball twisted in an orbit around the spinning wheel.

The table waited, silently.

It was the only thing silent in the casino. The clatter of slot-machines attempted to out drown the bubbling of conversation, laughter, and the blasting blare of the lounge show. It was a struggle which none of the trio of noise-makers could ever win.

"Number 13," the man behind the wheel announced. Chips were stacked on his green chips on number 13.

"Cash them in," Dan said in a tired voice, picking up the Martini he'd been forced to buy himself. He downed the drink, gathered up his chips.

He walked through the crowd, searching out one of the other members of his little group. Elliott, Helen, Doris. They were somewhere in the surging, colorful, intoxicated crowd. Somewhere at the tables, or somewhere at the slots.

He found a Black Jack table that was too crowded to get to, where Elliott was sitting with a stack of silver dollars in front of him. Dan tried to get the writer's attention, but finally gave up.

It was a drag at the Vegas Hotels when the late shows are about to open. The crowd was waiting for the star attraction, one of the famous Clan members, Dean Martin, Joey Bishop, Sammy Davis, Jr., and, of course, Frank Sinatra. Everybody and their brother, sister, father, mother, and lover gathered into the hotel between shows. There was hardly room to move through the aisles.

Cursing under his breath, Dan was just about to give up his hopeless search when he spotted Doris Patton pulling the handle of a slot machine. Stepping up beside her, Dan said: "How's winnings?"

"Terrible," Doris announced. Her eyes looked into his, then smiled. "Can I talk to you?"

"Sure," Dan told her.

She pulled the arm at the side of the machine one time more. The three cylinders whooshed around and around and around. They would sing either blues or rich man's booze. A cherry hit, the rest was a wash-out.

Doris picked up the three dimes and turned to Dan. "How about a drink?"

"Great idea."

They stepped into the cocktail lounge that was crowded around the lighted stage on which a combo was playing progressive jazz. It was a break between the entertainment portions of the lounge show. For that Dan was thankful. It would have been difficult to talk over some singing comic or vocal group blasting over the speakers.

They found a small circular table, sat down and stared at each other.

"We've come a long way," Doris said, smiling, her eyes searching his.

Dan nodded. They had. Their affair had burned bright—sensually bright—for a little while, then suddenly simmered down. But they had remained good friends. Doris was a good kid.

"How you enjoying yourself, Doris?"

She didn't get a chance to answer because the cocktail waitress came up for their order. The waitress was dressed like all the others: tights and leotards with a low-cut, bulging neckline.

Dan ordered a couple of Martinis, but Doris corrected him. "Make mine Scotch."

"Scotch? That's Elliott's joy-ride," Dan said after the waitress had left.

"He's a nice guy, Dan, isn't he?" Her question was more desperately probing than he would have thought necessary.

"A nice guy." He sipped his drink and they sat there for a long time, listening to the music.

Finally Doris sighed, gulped down half her Scotch and leveled her gaze on Dan.

"I like Elliott, Dan...but I'm afraid of him." She leaned across the small table, her eyes intense, her expression squeezed with concern. She pursed her lips in thought. "I like him a lot—but where's he aiming?"

Dan had an impulse to tell her that Elliott had asked the same kind of question about her. Then he realized that neither Doris nor Elliott would actually like that. Elliott had come in private. The man wouldn't want Doris to know that. Doris wouldn't

86

want Dan to tell Elliott about what was happening right then.

"What you worrying about?" Dan countered, taking another sip of his Martini, fingering the olive.

"I don't think he's a settling down kind. He chases around...been doing so for a long time. Oh, he has a good line—and I'll admit that I wouldn't mind being taken in...but I've been around too long, Dan, to be a fool...only thing—sometimes I wonder if he isn't really quite serious." She frowned for a moment, then smiled. "He came out the other night and said he was ready to settle down with the right girl...and right there he broke into a grin, and told me that I surely fit the bill. You know Elliott, some- times he's hard to take seriously. Only thing...hell, Dan—I don't know what's wrong with me, but I'm falling for the lug. I never enjoyed myself so much—never really wanted to settle down with any guy, until I met Elliott—I mean...got a chance to see him in his more serious moments. He can be really nice. The trouble is—the moment Elliott gets seri- ous he breaks off into that...hellish personality Sam bit. I would just like to see him get serious and stay serious long enough for me to know for sure!" She swallowed the rest of her Scotch, made a face and then laughed. "Didn't think little old Doris could fall, did you?"

Dan patted the woman's hand, affectionately. He felt like an older brother to Doris, and suddenly he was happy for her. The poor thing was suffering for nothing, though.

He was about to tell Doris that Elliott had indi- cated serious intentions, when the man stepped up to their table, grinning, clattering silver dollars in his bulging pockets. He chuckled, pulled up a chair from one of the other tables and said:

"Hi, folks." He kissed Doris lightly on the cheek. "How's the sweetheart?"

"Fine, Elliott. How'd you make out?"

"Even-Steven...just even-Steven!" he grinned, looking at Dan. "What you trying to do—take my girl away from me?"

"After all, Elliott, she's *my* secretary!" Dan winked at Doris.

She winked back, but her eyes were searching; questioning him.

He tried to show her by his expression that everything was perfect, but wasn't sure if the message got across.

"Why don't you get lost?" Elliott suggested. "Or get a girl of your own?"

"Seen her, by the way?" Dan inquired.

"The last time I saw Helen, she was playing craps. There's a girl who really swings the dice— you should have seen her. Hell, yelling—sorry," he quickly said to Doris, "I forgot myself."

"I swear once a year, too," Doris grinned, her eyes meeting Dan's for only a moment.

"Well, anyway, Helen's stacking them up! Both the chips and the men's eyes. You should see those guys, looking at that neckline of hers. Reminds me of the joke about the girl who came into the casino, walked up to the roulette table, put down her chips. She opened her fur coat just as the dice were thrown. She had nothing on underneath. She picked up all the chips on the table and rushed out. One dealer asked the other: 'Did she make her point?' and the other said, 'I don't know, I thought you were looking!'" Elliott laughed and the others joined in.

Dan finished his cocktail, said good-bye and headed for the dice table.

Helen was still there, stacking the chips in front of her, the men were still enjoying the view her low-cut, pink dress gave as she threw the dice, and squealed at them to make her point.

Dan tapped her on the shoulder.

"Not now, honey," she said, hardly looking up at him.

He didn't bother pushing. Helen had a fever that only time would wash out—or losing.

Idly he walked around the casino, stopped at several tables, almost played and decided it wasn't worth it. They'd been there for a night and day already and he hadn't slept yet. After work, Friday, they'd had dinner together, picked up their luggage, drove to the airport and arrived in Vegas a few hours later. After drinks in Elliott and Doris's room, they'd split up. Dan and Helen had circled the casino, playing at the tables together. By late morning both of them had returned to their rooms, discovered each other bodies, rested, without sleeping, gone out, had breakfast, and started gambling in a serious way until four in the afternoon. When they'd returned to their room, they called Elliott and Doris, had dinner with them, spilt up into twos, then singles, and now he was moving like a hypnotized zombie, dazed, exhausted beyond the ability of his nerves to understand how tired they were.

That was Vegas: a twenty-four-hour rampage without stop.

Dan decided to return to his room.

When he fell on the bed, his nerves were so tired that he didn't even feel his body hit the bed. Darkness seemed to take command sometime between the moment he started dropping and the time he hit.

* * * * * * *

Gale and Mildred had gone to Santa Monica. The sun was high, and hot.

Gale had worn her semi-bikini that attracted enough attention on the beach to make her glow inwardly. It was a white bikini which sliced across her stomach low enough to center her naval in dark tan flesh. The top piece covered the lower line of her breasts, and hid the color of her nipples; but hardly more.

Late in the afternoon, they left, had a dinner with cocktails, and returned to their apartment.

The sand, the burn which had tingled into her flesh during the afternoon, sent Gale into the shower without waiting to say anything to Mildred. She merely walked into the apartment, into the bathroom, slipped out of her bikini, turned on the shower, waited a moment for the water to get warm, and then stepped into the small stall, closing the glass door.

She was humming when a slight click sounded. She continued humming, in a world all her own. The needle spray of water tingled over her flesh like caressing tiny fingers. She thought about Dan Blair, as she had been doing for the last few days. Soon, very soon, she would be out with Dan. Every time she thought about that afternoon she had called the man, it was impossible not to blush. But the argument that made it possible to overcome the blush was the fact he'd offered to take her out.

The shower door suddenly opened.

Without a word, Mildred stepped in next to Gale.

"What the hell," Gale cried, surprised. She turned and before either of them could say anything more, their bodies were pressed together. The smallness of the shower stall made it impossible to not touch each other; and Mildred circled Gale's body with her arms, hugging close.

"Hi honey! Surprised?" Mildred's lips touched Gale's.

Their wet bodies slipped against one another and Gale felt a flush of pleasure at the texture of Mildred's flesh. It was different in the wetness. Delightfully different.

Their wet bodies clung together, the slippery flesh fusing, then jerking free.

She was gasping as they broke away from one another.

"We can't in here...can't!"

Gale felt the need for something more, something more complete. Gale knew that her need for something more than what Mildred, or all the Mildred's in the world, could give her, would drive her into the arms of Dan Blair. And that was both thrilling and frightening.

But what would the man think of her? she wondered, as they stepped out of the shower stall. *Of her being with Mildred?*

What difference did it make what he thought of her? Gale told herself. If they went out together and ended up in bed, it wouldn't affect her chances as an actress one way or the other.

She had a right to a life!

Both women went through the ritual of drying each other. It was a play-game they did automatically.

Later, after a couple of high-balls, Gale found herself allowing Mildred to make passes, and allowing her own body to return the caresses.

In the fire of the final moments of their love-making, Gale managed to blur out all thoughts, and afterwards was relieved to discover sleep came easily to her exhausted mind and body.

Her last dim thought was wondering how the *Chambers Steak House Cocktail Lounge* was getting along without her on Sunday night. At least, they hadn't made any fuss when she'd said it wasn't possible to make it that night for "personal reasons."

CHAPTER TEN

Monday morning.

This was the place, and Gale could hardly believe it. This was her personal Hollywood. Her first step into the world of dreams.

Crammed into one small studio lot west of La Brea on Santa Monica Boulevard was *her* Hollywood.

All Gale could think about was the fleecy cloud of excitement which kept following her as she stepped up to the guard who sat like some cruel ogre keeping unwanted "fans" off the lot.

"I'm supposed to report to Studio B," Gale told the stone faced man.

"Your name?"

"Gale Ross."

"Just a moment." A moment later, which seemed an endless eternity, the guard smiled, and the world smiled, because the world was now open to her. "It's down to the left, just keep going, you'll find a big white sign, black on white. That's Stage B. Across from the Commissary.... Working on the *Henderson City Story?*"

"I guess so," Gale beamed, finding it hard to keep the excitement out of her voice, off her face.

"New at the game?" the man inquired with a fatherly grin.

"Yes, isn't it wonderful?" She floated across the thin, invisible barrier that divided the professional from the fan. She was still floating as she started down the walkway toward Stage B.

How long had she struggled? How many nights and days, weeks—months, years, had her dream kept her going, sometimes desperately, sometimes casually, sometimes even almost forgetting, but continuing to dream, and hunger to discover the Hollywood that existed only in the dreams of young people seeking fame and fortune on the silver screen?

Hollywood glamour; and harsh reality.

You're just in a bit part, she kept telling herself. *It doesn't make you a star.*

But she felt *like a star.*

Gale looked around, trying to see if she could spot any real stars. Holly Hill was the studio's large, giant name. Wouldn't it be wonderful if she saw Holly Hill?

After all the partying, all the boozing, all the running away from grasping, hungry hands, greedy lips that offered so much for so little. Sleep with me, sweetheart, and the heavens are yours. Hell, they were! Sleep and only the gutter was hers.

She rounded a corner, saw the large white, square sign with the beautiful plain black lettering announcing:

STAGE B

She looked for an entrance, expecting glittering gold, inlaid with diamonds, emeralds, pearls. Nothing. Just a plain, green double door.

This certainly couldn't be the entranceway to Heavenly stardom.

The cloud disintegrated. She stood there, ten feet from the sound stage door, in the middle of nowhere, scared, frightened, because she didn't know what to do. Everything seemed so damned silent this time in the morning. Eight in the morning, and everything was quite. Maybe she'd made a mistake? Maybe they weren't really shooting today.

Then she remembered the guard and what he had said.

The door opened and a man stepped outside, lighted a cigarette and looked at her. He grinned "Hello!"

"Is this the set for the...*Henderson Story?*" she asked in a voice that was as unsure as the butterflies in her stomach were churning harsh uncertainty.

"Sure. You looking for it? Go on in." He made a movement of his arm, inviting. Then his attention disappeared, faded. He watched her step forward, but his eyes were vague, distant.

She walked into the dimly lighted sound stage, almost stumbled over an electric cord, and caught herself in time. Froze. Stood there listening.

Sound. Sound that had no real shape at first. There was a loud murmuring of voices in the distance, across the huge warehouse type building; across in a world of make-believe that seemed far too real, far too terrifying.

Bodiless voices were muttering cracks of sound:
"Hey, hit that broad!"
"Over a little to the right...hold it—"
"Dolly in a bit..."

"That's good."

"Look, sweetheart, just do it the way we ran through it. Don't try to ad-lib..."

"Get a reading on the lights—"

"Will the make-up guy get over here—her face is too shiny...come on—step on it!"

"Don't you think I should hold my hand this way, Darling?"

"Sweetheart, like we ran through it. Just don't ad-lib!"

"That broad—I said hit her—and now."

"Damn it—who moved that light. Put it back, some...body!"

"Sweetheart, you look wonderful—Make-up man—fix her face—the lights shine on it. Don't worry about anything, Sweetheart—come on, make-up!"

"Pan to the left—that's the way the script calls for it...not so damned far! Okay, that's better...no, just a hair more—okay, mark that out."

Sounds. Sounds that terrified and excited at the same time. All those voices, shouting, screaming at each other.

"Who are you?" a voice question at her side.

Gale turned, looked at the thin faced man who had stepped into the building behind her.

"I'm Gale Ross."

"What is that?" The man's narrow face pinched tighter, bringing the eyes closer together.

"I was told to come here, today. Dan Blair's office sent me."

"Yeah, of course. But what're you playing?"

"I don't really know. He didn't say! Just said to report to the...studio." Suddenly she wanted to cry,

96

and didn't understand why.

"Okay, come with me...I'll introduce you to Dave, our director—he probably knows what to do with you." The man took her arm. Introduced himself: "I'm Jimmy Stone...work in the script department. Come on!" He pulled her after him. "Watch out for the lights. Just don't touch anything. That's the first thing you'll have to learn around here. Don't touch anything. Dave will scream his head off—Johnny, our camera-man, will blow the ceiling off...but you'll learn fast."

"Is he the one who's yelling to hit the woman?"

"What?"

"Hitting the broads!"

"Oh," he chuckled. "That's a word for a light... not a woman!"

"Oh...."

"Don't worry...you'll learn it all, after a while!"

"What makes you think I don't know?" she demanded haughtily. "Just because I made a joke...."

"Okay, funny joke," the man generously offered, obviously not believing the flub about the "broads" being a joke.

"But we all had to start from the beginning, and learn the ground rules," was his only explanation.

Did it show *that much?* Gale wondered.

She was pushed through a series of dark, silently, resting lights, around boxes, over thick cords, and finally to the set. It was the main street of a small middle class, mid-western town, too much like the one she'd grown up in. For a moment she felt confused and imagined herself back home, the *Temple Theater* down the street, where she'd spent so many Saturday afternoons looking at the movies.

The illusion shattered as a bull-necked man with white hair over his forehead, thrust his face at hers.

"Who are you?" the man demanded.

"Dave, this is...."

"Gale Ross," she quickly offered.

"Yeah, Gale Ross," Jimmy introduced. "Dan sent her down—where do I put her?"

Dave swung his hands in the air, looked at the heavens and groaned: "How the hell do I know? Call Dan—maybe he knows!"

Dave peered at her for a moment then grinned. "You're lovely, sweetheart."

Then he forgot her as he turned to the woman on the set, standing at the corner of a drug store, men hustling around her like bees fighting for honey. "Okay, sweetheart you look beautiful—want to run through it again for me? Just like before."

Gale wanted to watch, but Jimmy pulled her away, back around the large camera, to the left of the Henderson City set. They came to a small phone booth. He picked up a receiver and demanded Dan Blair's office. "I want him to call—where's his secretary? Out, too? Oh, hell!" Jimmy turned, shrugged at Gale and then went back to the set, as if already forgetting her.

Gale followed the man, watched as the young actress went through the motions as the director instructed her.

The woman looked to the right and then to the left, frowned, then ran off the set, screaming.

Dave groaned. "Okay, try it again. Look really terrified. He's after you. Jack-the-Ripper—the Devil—anything you want to think of! Just try to image the most horrible creature in the world is after you. Look scared...you're running for your life. Now do it again sweetheart!"

Dave made a face at the cameraman, shrugged bull shoulders and turned his attention toward the girl

Gale watched while the woman went through the routine a half a dozen times. At the end of each run through Dave would scream at her to do it again.

Gale wished she could have a chance at it. She was sure it would be a simple matter to please the director, Dave. But this wasn't for her. All she could do was watch the woman vainly try to appear frightened.

The way Gale felt it wouldn't be hard to act frightened. She was scared to death.

Finally, Dave tired of trying to make his "Sweetheart" do it perfectly and announced the next time would be a take.

After the make-up men had worked over the woman's face, Dave turned to the surrounding crew.

"Quiet, now—this is a take!"

A slate boy slid in front of the camera. Snap went the slate. The boy disappeared.

"Okay, sweetheart, do your stuff!"

The woman went though the routine, her face contorted to the required actions, her voice screamed at just the right time and then her feet took her off the set.

"Cut!" Dave turned in Gale's direction, mumbling to nobody in particular, "Who the hell did that bitch sleep with?"

His eyes spotted Gale and another moan uttered

from his barrel chest.

Gale knew he must be wondering the same thing about her. She tried to smile reassuringly to the man, but he wasn't paying the least bit of attention.

"Okay," Dave shouted, "let's try it once more, just for safety."

The scene was repeated, and then repeated again. By the fourth time Dave cursed under his breath, turned to the cameraman, said: "Okay, Johnny, let's break for lunch. No sense wasting any more footage on this bit. If we don't have some-thing—hell, we *have* to have it! We can't spend all day on this one stupid scene!"

He turned back to the woman, walked to her side, grinned: "Okay, sweetheart, that was fine...you change for the next scene—and we'll strike this set." He addressed the whole sound stage: "Be back at one-thirty."

As Dave passed Gale, she stopped him with: "Who am I supposed to report to?"

He looked at Gale as if seeing her for the first time.

"You're beautiful, sweetheart." He started away.

"Where should I report to?" she yelled after him.

"Hell, I don't know!" he shouted back.

Jimmy came up to her, smiled understandingly. "He's a good sort, but has problems. Carrie Eaton—that's the girl, is a spike in his...head—he has to di-rect her through the pilot and...well, he has big prob-lems. Had arguments with the head office about Miss Eaton—but she's in solid with somebody. And that's it. Can I take you to lunch—then we can look up Mr. Blair and find out what you're supposed to be doing."

Gale hesitated and then smiled. "Well, thanks, Jimmy."

They went to the Commissary to eat.

CHAPTER ELEVEN

Dan drove to Helen's place first, waited until the woman changed, then they went to his apartment, where he changed. It was eleven by the time he put his jacket on.

"How about a drink, first—before heading back to the studio?"

Helen nodded.

They finished their highballs, then went to his car.

"Van Houten will have missed you," Dan said, as they drove into his parking space.

"Hell, he's out of town today—did you forget—up in Frisco."

They walked across the parking lot, through the Studio gate, nodded to the guard, and then went their own ways. He walked to the Commissary, groaned at the crowd that had gathered there to eat, waited in line until he could pick out some beef stew, got coffee and then carried his tray across the crowded room.

Dan was about to sit down when he spotted a face that stopped him in mid step.

There she was, sitting a couple of tables away from him, with Jimmy Stone. For a moment Dan

102

didn't remember who she was. He only knew that she was beautiful, then he remembered her. At that same moment Jimmy caught his eye, smiled, and nodded.

Dan moved to the table.

"Hello, Miss Ross," Dan said, sitting down between them.

She said: "Oh, you *do* remember me. We'd just decided that maybe you hadn't."

Dan turned to Jimmy. "What's the trouble?"

"We don't know what to do with her." The man's eyes grinned, indicating that *he* knew what he would like to do with Gale.

Dan felt annoyed. He wanted to be rid of Jimmy, but didn't say anything about it.

He turned, looked at Gale. "What happened?"

"Nothing—I got here on time, but nobody seems to know what to do with me." She shrugged, tried to smile, but didn't quite make it.

Poor girl, Dan thought, *nervous as hell!* Her big moment and there was nobody here to give it to her.

"Didn't Dave...oh, hell, I bet we didn't tell him. Anyway—you're supposed to play opposite Miss Eaton this afternoon. It should have been this morning, but if I know Dave—she probably ran through the morning bit half a dozen times...or more!"

"What's with her?" Jimmy asked. "She can't act her way out of a paper bag!"

Dan shrugged. "Oh, come on—Jimmy—it's not really that bad. She's okay—only thing, Dave is...well, fussy. He wants everything to be perfect. Dave's a damned good director. He shouldn't be working on this hack stuff. He doesn't have the personality for it."

"Who's pushing Miss Eaton?" Jimmy wanted to know.

Dan frowned. "I wasn't aware anybody was."

"Oh, come on, Dan, don't pull my leg. You know as well as I do that somebody is giving her a push-job...who?" Jimmy nudged Dan in the arm.

"I picked her out for the part because she looks like Loni Blake—the role fit. She acts well enough. Dave screamed his head off—but I said she stays—and that's it!" Dan was telling the truth, basically. Carrie Eaton could act as well as any other hack actress sleeping with the studio boss. He had picked her out only because she fit the role of Lori Blake. And because she might be groomed to second Holly Hill at the studio; a promotion that took time and money. Acting talent was second to looks. The cutting room was where all the bad stuff got put together in a string that looked good, the rest landed on the floor and stayed there until somebody swept it up. With the right cutting and the right PR it was possible to make anybody look good. So Carrie Eaton had been picked. He'd seen some of her clips and she could be made to look pretty okay. That's all that mattered in the end.

The part Gale was to have carried only a few lines—Miss Eaton was being featured. In the long run, Gale's part could be cut out of the film, without too much effort. In fact, no effort at all.

He looked at Gale, said: "We better move, and fast. You should have been in make-up...they have to fix you up—" Turning to Jimmy, he asked, "When's shooting?"

"One-thirty."

Dan glanced at the commissary clock. "Christ—

forty minutes. You won't make it!" He dragged Gale to her feet. "Come on, honey...sorry, no time to finish. If you aren't on that set on time, Dave will cook me alive—and your life won't be worth living for the next few hours."

He dragged her through the crowded room, outside, across the lot and into unmarked building.

They didn't stop running until she fully clothed in a pink sweater, gray skirt, her hair done up on her head in a pony-tail, and on onto Stage B.

As Dan returned to his office, he was thinking about Gale, wondering what it would be like to date her, to make love to that wonderful looking body. For one moment, in the make-up room, he'd seen her in a slip, and that short glimpse of her fired his imagination and desire. She was lovelier than he'd imagined.

Doris cut into his thoughts. "Holly called. Mad as hell. She wants you to call her *at once*—at her home."

"Okay, put the call through," he sighed, going into his inner office.

Sitting down at the desk, he waded through his thoughts, trying to figure out some way he might be able to soothe Holly Hill's temper.

The buzzer rang at his desk, and Dan picked up the receiver.

"Hello, darling," he greeted.

"Hello, darling, nothing!" Holly snapped. 'Where were you? I tried to call you all weekend...I had plans, you bastard!"

"I couldn't help it, Holly. Had to go out of town on business—"

"Business? Hell you did. I checked around...just

to make sure!" Holly's voice was high pitch, grating, near hysteria.

"On pleasure."

"Pleasure?" She gagged out over the receiver.

"Had to rest up..." He tried to laugh. "You're a real bulldozer, Holly. You gotta give a guy a break, now and then. Hell, you've been running me ragged...I love it, baby, but...try to understand. You are fantastic, but you drain a man's brain and body. I mean, honey, when you're doin' me I'm bombed out of my mind!"

There was hesitation and then Holly laughed back at him. "Maybe you're right...come up, tonight?"

"Can't wait!" he lied.

* * * * * * *

Gale was drunk with happiness.

"I'm so happy for you," Mildred breathed, surging closer. "I'd do anything for you...Gale."

"Yes...thanks to you..." Gale hugged Mildred to her. Tonight everything was different. Tonight everything was in beautiful color. Beautiful colors that flashed, "GALE ROSS, STAR!"

Mildred was talking to her and for a long time she wasn't aware of what the woman said.

Then the words started to come into sharper focus, as if coming closer and closer from faraway.

"...and I'll always need you, Gale...there isn't a thing I wouldn't do for you...ever—except give you up. I couldn't stand that...I couldn't stand the idea of you being out of my life, forever...promise you won't leave me, Gale...promise me."

The woman's body clung closer, greedily. "Promise me."

"I can't, Milly...I can't..." Gale felt sick inside at the very thought of not ever finding that kind of the love and beauty that had been hers with Wayne. "I need something more than just this, Milly! It isn't your fault...this can't last..."

There was a stony silence and then Mildred Mason sat up, glaring down at Gale.

"I won't let you leave, Gale. If you try...I'll see to it you don't ever get a job in Hollywood—ever!"

The woman's eyes were harsh, cold, threatening.

"Please, Milly..."

"I mean it, Gale...I'll tell Frankie to call it off—I'll tell him to cut all lines...and make sure you don't get work through him—and that Van Houten gives the...well, we won't talk about it...this is a celebration—not a death watch!"

Mildred reached for the glass on the night stand next to her. She saluted, laughed, said: "Let's celebrate!"

Gale frowned, then attempted to forget what the woman had threatened. Maybe it was only drunk talk. In any case, how much damage could Frankie do? He was only her agent. There were other agents. Could a guy like him do *that* much damage? Maybe. Maybe not.

The rest of the night was unsettling for Gale. She couldn't make up her mind how serious Mildred Mason's threat could be. Gale found her mind worrying over the torment of her need for a man, a career and Mildred Mason's very real sounding threat.

SEX QUEEN, BY CHARLES NUETZEL

CHAPTER TWELVE

The next morning Dan came to the office exhausted from his evening with Holly Hill. It had been a rat race nightmare.

His throat was sore and dry and the need for some kind of liquor brought out the small pint of whiskey from his lower left drawer. He sat there, behind his desk, trying to soothe the raw places where Holly had marked him the night before.

She was too intense for any one man, Dan realized, taking a gulp of the whiskey. How much longer would she demand his services? Her endless demands were bringing him to the limit of his physical and emotional endurance.

Doris came into his office, smiled, and then frowned at his face.

"You look hung over." Her eyes caught the open bottle in his hand

"Want a swallow?" he offered.

She laughed. "No, not this early in the morning. Want to tell 'Mother' all about it?"

"You wouldn't understand." He looked at the papers in her hands. "Work?"

"Just sign them. I'll take them to the accounting office."

He signed until he came to the order on Gale Ross.

"When are the rushes, today?" he asked, handing the papers to his secretary.

"Same as usual. Ten." She frowned once more at him. "Sure I won't understand?"

"About what?"

"Your troubles." She studied him for a moment and then shrugged. "If you need a solid feminine ear, come to me, lover."

"Thanks. I'll remember."

He was busy at ten and didn't make the rushes, but later that day Dave called his office.

"Want to see you, have something interesting, Dan."

"What about?"

"Wait till you see, sweetheart," Dave shouted over the receiver. "I got something that's pure gold. You have time?"

"Important?"

"Important enough. You know that girl you brought over yesterday afternoon—the one that did the scene with Carrie?"

"What about her?"

"That's it. Come on over to projection room 5 . . right away?"

Dan didn't bother to check with Doris about appointments. "Be right over."

On his way past Doris' desk, he said: "Hold appointments for thirty minutes...no...until I tell you."

The projection room was dark, quiet. Dave Kroph sat next to Dan, breathing hard. Then the big man leaned forward, picked up the phone in front of him, said: "Hurry on that film, Eddy."

Something clicked in the booth behind them. Light sprayed on the screen.

8-7-6-5-4-3-2 flashed on, then the slate board with "Hen City, Sc. 107, Take 1," slapped on the screen.

"Watch this, Dan," Dave said.

The scene was a living room, furnished plain, Carrie "Lori Blake" Eaton stood up from a chair as the young blonde walked in, slouched onto the sofa.

"Debra," Eaton scolded, "won't you ever learn to be a lady!"

Debra's voice said, from behind the sofa's back, "That ain't nothin' to do with bein' no lady!"

"Oh, Debra, cut that out!" Eaton said in a flat, irritated voice.

Dave's voice, off camera cursed, "Cut!"

The slate said the same thing, except this was Take 2.

The scene repeated itself.

"Debra" walked onto the scene, plunked down, repeated, in the same, nasal voice, "That ain't nothin' to do with bein' no lady!"

Eaton said, "Oh, Debra, cut that out!"

The scene continued.

"Debra" stood from the sofa, glared at Eaton, her chest heaving, then said in a girlishly cultured voice:

"Won't you ever learn that being a lady has nothing to do with the way a girl relaxes on a sofa? Oh, I'll never understand you!"

The girl left the room, slamming the door behind her. Eaton stood there for a moment, turned toward the camera, and then sighed.

The screen went blank.

Dave said: "What do you think?"

"You better cut it out of the film."

"What!" Dave exploded, standing in the darkness and looking down at Dan.

"I said cut it out—or reshoot with another girl."

Dave sputtered and slammed his fist against the arm of the chair. "Damn it, Dan—that's the best goddamned scene in the picture—the show. That woman can *act!* Really *act.* Where've you been keeping her?"

Dan knew he was grinning, grinning happily and not really knowing why. Gale Ross, as Debra, had stolen the scene completely. She was too good.

"You know why, Dave," Dan said as the lights turned on. "We can't have it in—it makes Carrie look like a rank amateur."

After a moment Dave's face relaxed from the harsh red steel it had become. He sighed loud, long. "Yes...I guess you are right...guess I knew it, too. But what about the girl?"

"What about her? You're the director."

"Is she signed up with the studio?"

"No."

"Oh, God! Sign her—for god's sake—and mine—sign her. What she did with a no-bit walk-on...hell, I'd like to see what she'd do with a real blood and guts part!"

"I can't sign anybody to a studio contract, and you know it, Dave." Dan sat there thinking, feeling an excitement that he'd never felt before while working in the studios. Gale Ross could more than act. It was magic, the kind that reached out and grabbed you where it did the most good. At first he hadn't even thought of Debra as Gale Ross. It had been Debra, the little sister to Lori Blake. The scene had merely been there to show what a snob Lori was. But Gale Ross had grabbed it, completely. If the scene stayed, it would ruin the whole hour. Gale had the magic element that made the difference between middle-class hack and Big-Name Star. Where she had been keeping it, Dan would never know.

"Did you show Murry?" Dan wanted to know.

"Not yet. I wanted you to see it. This morning...well, I managed to miss the rushes, learned you hadn't seen them, from Greg—he's assisting me, you know."

"I know."

"Well, when Greg raved about this...what's her damned name?"

"Gale Ross."

"Gale Ross, I thought he was out of his head. He had to drag me here. I've been looking through the five takes, and every damned one she's the same— not a difference...oh, maybe a little, here and there—but basically the same. And I only had to explain one time. Just once to her. Yesterday I didn't have time to notice. Today—I remembered— notice and salute. When do we show Murry?"

"I'll arrange it." Dan stood, patted Dave on the shoulder. "Thanks—I think maybe I'll have some fun with this." He flicked his eyes toward the screen. "She's a pretty little woman.'

"Little, hell, great, damned great, and *what* a woman! Watching her work is a pleasure I won't forget."

Dave was still raving as Dan walked out of the projection booth.

He walked around the studio lot several times,

112

smoking one cigarette after another.

Stepping into Murry Van Houten's office, Dan asked Helen if the big man was in.

"He's still out—remember, Dan?" She frowned. "What's wrong?"

Dan groaned. "Damn that Frisco trip!"

Without a word he slammed the door behind him, returned to his office. He told Doris to get Gale Ross on the phone and told her to get Dave Kroph, first, and tell the man to hide that film, and keep it hidden until ordered otherwise. Minutes later, Doris said she had Gale Ross on the line.

"Hello, Gale?" Dan said.

"Oh, hello, Mr. Blair."

"Dan...Dan, honey," he instructed. "You doing anything tonight?"

Hesitation and then : "No."

"Well, I'll pick you up at...seven-thirty...for dinner. "Okay?"

"Of course. Of course." Hesitation, then: "How'd I make out yesterday?"

He was tempted to tell her, but caution held him off. "I don't know, I'll find out from Dave."

They said good-bye, and as he hung up the phone, Dan remembered he was supposed to go over to Holly Hill's home that evening.

To hell with Holly! he decided.

"Doris, get Miss Hill on the phone—no ...you call her up, say I'm out of town—anything...just say I can't make it tonight."

With that, he sat there for the rest of the afternoon trying to plan on how he would handle Gale Ross's career if he got the chance.

CHAPTER THIRTEEN

Gale knew she was making too much of a fuss over her make-up. She fiddled with the lipsticks, trying to figure out which color would look best. *Pink Coral, Passion Pink, Crimson, Blood Love, Pale Red Coral, Orange Sunset, or what...?*

She had wiggled into a red sheath that showed her figure off to the best advantage. The neckline opened wide at the shoulders, and dipped low in the middle. Gale studied herself, dabbed perfume between her breasts, behind her ears. She had let her hair fall over her shoulders to appear casual; but it had taken over an hour to set it just right.

Butterflies had been fluttering along the lining of her stomach. A quick shot of brandy had soothed them down for a short while, long enough to shower, set her hair, wait, dress.

Now the butterflies were fluttering angrily again!

She decided on Blood Love, which was just off red, with a tinge of orange mixed with it. That would go with her hair and dress.

The image in the mirror pursed its lips, then spread them wide over gleaming white teeth. They were her own, natural teeth, not capped, like Mildred's. She had always been proud of her teeth; and of her lips and figure.

Now, Gale felt uncertain. She was frightened to death. It was more than the fact that Dan Blair was Dan Blair, Casting Director for *Henderson City;* and strangely it was more than the fact that he was the first man she'd gone out with since Wayne Gilman's death.

If he made a pass, would she allow it to be completed? And maybe for the wrong reasons? Last night she'd been so sure. Gale puzzled over that thought for a long time, the lipstick held in her hand, only inches from her full lush lips.

"You're certainly making a fuss over this *man,*" Mildred observed from the bed, where she'd settled down after showering. Naked, her hand was cupped under one hefty breast. "I don't see why you give such a damn!"

Gale snapped out of her daze, started lining her lips.

"I wish you were staying home, honey—you'll get home early, won't you?" Mildred was saying.

Gale looked at the woman's reflection in the mirror.

Mildred laid there, her legs slipped under her, her breasts supported by two delicate hands. The look in the woman's eyes was open wanting, and something else that Gale couldn't quite place.

"Why fuss, so, honey?" Mildred snapped suddenly.

"I'm not fussing."

"Oh, I've watched you all...for two hours, fussing, and fussing, as if the guy really meant something to you." Mildred's words were sharp, edged almost with hatred. "He's just a john, so to speak. Somebody to use! A connection. Business. Not some romantic seduction! And that's the way you're acting. Like some school kid fixing up for her first date with a guy she has a childish crush on!"

"Don't be silly, Milly, after all, he *is* an important man at the studio!" She pressed her lips together, working the Blood Love over their lush surfaces.

"Oh, come on, now, honey, you know he doesn't mean shit—not *really!* Frankie, your agent, has the in with Van Houten and...and you didn't have to play up to him!"

"And Dan Blair could just be the padlock that will make it a sure thing!" Gale snapped, irritated by the conversation; irritated by Mildred's tone.

"You make me sick!" Mildred snapped back, flinging her legs over the edge of the bed. "You act just as if you were...actually *interested* in the man."

"And what if I am?" Gale countered, turning, glaring at her roommate.

Mildred's eyes narrowed, then her lips laughed, harshly. "Oh, come on, honey, after what we've meant to each other. You couldn't be *serious!*"

The expression on the other woman's face shriveled up the retort that had trembled on Gale's lips. After a moment she shrugged. "Well, what if I was?"

But her voice was light, as if kidding.

Silence. Then Mildred stepped over to Gale, slipped her hands around her chest, pressing underneath her neckline. "I don't know what I'd do...I need you, Gale. More than I've ever needed any other woman. I wish I'd never introduced you to

116

Frankie...I wish we could go off some place and...just be together forever."

Gale wanted to push the woman away; wanted to tell Mildred to keep her hands to herself, but she remained silent.

"I guess I love you, Gale...that's my trouble. I love you and don't want to lose you. Silly of me...hell, this Dan Blair can't mean anything to either of us...he couldn't come between us—not after all we've gone through together. I'm an ape!" She laughed nervously, but her eyes looked unsure, as if she were trying to convince herself with bold, confident words. "We're good for each other. I'm going to be glad when you get back tonight. I'll wait up—you'll be in early, won't you?"

"I imagine so..."

"Promise?"

She felt trapped. Maybe it had been a mistake getting involved with Mildred. In fact, on some levels, it had been. On the other hand, maybe things would just work themselves out.

The doorbell rang, saving Gale the necessity of promising anything.

"Oh, my god! Hold him off, will you, please. Just for me?" She hardly heard the other woman leaving the room to answer the doorbell.

* * * * * * *

Dan looked at the woman, found it hard not to notice that there couldn't be much under the robe hugging her hefty body. When she moved back, away from the door, the robe opened at the top, just slightly, and he was sure the woman was stark naked.

"I'm Mildred Mason," she breathed in a husky, inviting voice, her eyes flashing. "Gale will be a few moments. Can I fix you a drink?" she offered, closing the door behind him.

"Thanks."

She disappeared and returned with a Scotch and soda.

"Thought you were a Scotch man," she observed, standing over him, letting her eyes sweep his body as if mentally stripping him. It was a flirtatious action, yet seemed to miss any emotional cord; just raw, unfeeling sex.

"Why?" he countered, smiling.

"Oh, some guys look—well, classy. You look classy. Thus scotch!" Her eyes met his, this time quite obviously offering anything he might ask.

Dan found it hard not to laugh at Mildred. She was like a comic, making a take-off of a prostitute trying to interest a client.

He was glad when the bedroom door opened and Gale Ross stepped into the living room.

She stood there, staring across the room at him, a thin, shy smile working the corners of her lips upwards. They dimpled slightly, her eyes silently flirted with his. She was beautiful, hugged in crimson which thrust over the well supplied neckline, curved around generous, lovely hips. Her calves and ankles were perfectly formed, her feet almost delicate in the tiny looking, ultra high-heeled black shoes.

"How are you?" she asked in a soft whisper that seemed to reach across all that space and kiss the air in front of his lips.

He didn't dare tell her exactly how he was, because suddenly an immediate reaction tightened every muscle in him

She was lovelier than he had remembered. Or, Dan corrected the observation, maybe more beautiful than he'd noticed before.

He didn't even finish his drink; the mere vision of Gale was enough to make him feel very high. Absently he thanked Mildred, and stepped toward Gale.

"Well, shall we go?" he suggested, taking her arm. There wasn't any electric shock at contact, but a deliciously heady sense of pleasure that flowed through him.

They floated out of the apartment. At least, it seemed that way to Dan.

Suddenly he realized that it was going to be a more beautiful evening than he'd imagined. And his imagination had performed miracles with his mind all afternoon.

* * * * * * *

Mildred stared at the door as it closed behind the couple. A hard bitterness settled deep within her.

Hate that man! She hated him with every nerve in her body.

Her little flirting had been an attempt to hide that out right hatred.

Mixing herself a strong highball, Mildred settled in front of the television set, but not looking at the show flickering there. Her mind kept sinking deeper and deeper into depressive hatred. It was impossible to keep from thinking about the way that Dan Blair had looked at Gale. The thought of what that expression meant, so hot in the depths of the man's eyes, sent shivers over Mildred. It had been her hope that by introducing Gale to Frankie that it would be possible to keep her away from any awkward situations with men in the Industry. The agent had no interest in women, and he'd been told to get Gale in without having to spread sexual goodies to some slob SOB. The way that Gale had acted, all afternoon, and especially the way she'd looked back at Dan, created even a stronger emotional fuse throughout Mildred's mind and body.

She'd do anything to keep Gale from getting involved with a man. Any man! But especially Dan Blair.

It might be impossible to hold Gale; and Mildred was afraid of what would happen if she lost the woman. She'd known a lot of women in her time, but this young lady was special. Right off at first sight she'd been taken by her—love? Maybe it was the real thing.

Life without Gale...can't let it happen! Horrible...

But she wouldn't consider that thought, because there were ways to hold the woman; ways to see to it that Gale kept in line. And she was determined to do just that!

CHAPTER FOURTEEN

Somehow the evening was flying away, and for Gale it was a daze of colors, places, and sensations.

The way that Dan touched her, fired her nerves with electricity. Not exactly the same as that first time in his office, but delightfully exciting. The way he helped her out of the car, into a chair, the way he lighted her cigarette, gazing into her eyes as if stripping her soul bare. Or trying to reach deep into her soul, make a connection, blending them together in some kind of mystic universe all their own.

The places.

A restaurant with palm leaves, scented tropical winds breathing on the atmosphere, the flavor of the West Indies, the South Pacific. The *Islander* lived up to the name. Tropical bamboo setting, dark lighting, intimate atmosphere for two romancers on a south sea cruise. Tall, rum drinks tasted of fruited wind playing through gently swaying palm trees moving against the evening sunset. She could almost picture a beach beyond the restaurant walls, with the waves splashing up white sand and the gay laughter of lovers, hidden in the underbrush, as they experienced secret romantic interludes. Of course that last was illusion.

121

The food was excellent, but she hardly noticed. A glow had clouded her vision, her tastes, even the liquor didn't seem to make her drunk. She was intoxicated with happiness; with Dan!

They laughed, talked about everything and nothing. She didn't even listen to the words; she felt the sounds folding in around her, embracing every nerve. They were like delicious caresses that just wound around her very being, embracing every sense with murmuring love. And that's exactly how it seemed. It was as if this man were making love to her with every word—a crazy kind of love-making that was deeper than any sexual thing. It was madness. Heavenly caresses all over her very soul.

Then they were driving in the night. And in another part of the universe. Somewhere in the city, somewhere else, together and alone, even while the world flowed about them. She was so close that she could touch him. She moved closer, impulsively. It was like spinning within a wild vortex, just the two of them. As she touched him, her eyes closed as she quivered uncontrollably.

"Having fun?" he asked.

"Loads."

They were dancing in an intimate cocktail lounge, and he was saying: "I'm glad you are enjoying yourself, Gale."

Music swelled in gentle, powerful waves, flowing in and through their bodies, becoming a very part of their mutual universe. It was overwhelmingly beautiful, sensual and spiritual all at once, reaching down into the deepest pits of her very existence. They literally flowed in some magical wind of sound.

She thrilled to the touch of his body so close to hers. The maleness of him, pressing against her hips, gently moving in time with the music, excited her. She hugged slightly closer, looking up into his mysterious brown eyes and wondered what he was thinking.

Scenes seemed to shift, change, magically.

"I'm having more fun than I've had in weeks," he was saying over a cocktail in another place, another time, another mood.

"So am I," Gale breathed as they walked on the beach, in Santa Monica.

The wind breezed against her cheeks, chilly, cold. Yet she felt the fury of fires soothing every nerve, deeply flushing her total being. She leaned closer to the man walking beside her.

Strange, she didn't remembering coming to the beach. She didn't really remember much except the sensations, the endless searching of his eyes, probing deep into hers. Their very souls seemed to have met somewhere within that space in her mind, her inner being, flowing together into one mutually created universe.

The coolness of the breeze; the soft murmuring of the ocean playing gaily on the sands. The dim glow of the half-moon bathing down upon them from a sky of twinkling stars, had created a solidity to the moment, bringing it into sharp focus. Maybe because this was where they should have been, where they had started at the *Islander,* a thousand years ago, a mere breathe before this very instant.

They stood, looking out at the ocean, watching the waves break on the dark sands. They kicked off their shoes, treaded in the water. Laughed.

123

"You're crazy," he told Gale.

"What's wrong with being crazy?" she wanted to know.

"Nothing, nothing at all. It's delightful. Beautiful. You are so damned beautiful, Gale." He held her in his arms, the water circling around their ankles, the sky casting soft milky strokes on his handsome, dark features. His lips were almost touching hers. And then, they touched.

Oh, God, he's wonderful, Gale screamed in Gale's brain. *I could simply die in his arms and be in heaven. He's so wonderful! He's all I want in life.*

* * * * * * *

She's wonderful, Dan screamed in Dan's brain, as he covered her soft lips, thrilled to the velvet texture which trembled under his mouth.

Her body arched closer, her breasts, yielding, crushed against him, soft under the material of her dress and bra. He wanted to make love to her, love to her lips, to her beautiful blue eyes, to her long, silken hair. He desperately wanted to love every inch of her very soul, explore every cell, nerve, right down to the center of all that she was. He wanted to be joined to her personal universe. And devour every element that made up her total being. He wanted to envelop her forever in a mutual space into which nobody else could ever enter. He wanted her all to himself! It was far more than a mere physical need, hunger, or obsession.

He pulled her harder against him, feeling the firm pressure of her thighs against his own. Her lips opened, and he gently, carefully, explored the per-

124

fection of her as he felt the moist warmth of a tiny pointed tongue press against his own.

Then they came up for air, away from the sensual depths that had folded around them, parting, and simply stared at each other, breathlessly.

He looked at her, the wind blowing her hair out, waving it behind her head like silken gold, fluttering in slow motion. Her eyes glistened with emotion, her lips, moist and like rubies, glittered in the moonlight, parted, as if waiting for some magic to bring them to life.

I love you, Gale Ross, I really love you, Gale Ross, his mind chanted. *How could I not love you? How can any man not fall desperately in love with the very perfection of all that is you?*

But of course that was impossible. He loved the evening; he loved the moment that had wrapped itself gently, caressingly, completely, around him. He loved the feeling that ebbed up into existence as he looked into her eyes. He felt her soul reach out and touch his. He loved that instant in time that held so much beauty. It was an illusive moment, eternal in itself, and yet a swift flash of perfection which couldn't possibly exist in the real universe. It was pure, beautiful, perfect illusion, nothing more.

But love Gale Ross, a girl he didn't even know? That was certainly impossible.

And such a delicious idea. Two souls meeting and blending and becoming one for eternity. But that was hardly reality; mere fantasy.

Dan laughed, gripped hold of her hand and they ran up, out of the water.

He looked at her as she bent over, putting her shoes on the stockinged legs.

"They're ruined," he said.

"I can get new stockings. It was worth it." She smiled and then slowly stood.

They walked back to the car without saying another word. Once inside, the world shut out, he offered her a cigarette, took one for himself, and lighted both.

They sat there for a long time, each on their own side of the car, miles apart, trapped in their own thoughts, their own world of confusion.

He wondered what she thought of him. Surely that expression on her face was a good job of acting. Gale's eyes silently spoken of love, romance, and all things that man would desire in a woman; they were skilled at saying exactly what she must have wanted them to say. But surely they were merely acting out the emotions her mind put in them. A false illusion. What else could it be?

He had no doubt concerning her acting ability. And she had certainly fed him a full course of it throughout the whole evening, leaving him breathless. What a magic power she would have on the screen. That kind of acting was beyond magic; it touched reality, stroking it with loving care, and then enveloped it to her very soul. That was such a wonderful illusion.

Yes, it was a beautiful evening. *Too* beautiful.

He looked at his watch.

"You know," Dan said, "It's past four."

"Oh, my God, you're kidding!" Gale put out the cigarette, turned her eyes toward him. "You *must* be kidding."

He shrugged, started the car.

Dan wanted to stop some place, find a room,

126

and make passionate love to Gale. But he passed the motels along the way. He wondered why, as he parked the car outside Gale's apartment.

They moved into each other's arms, without a word, without warning, as if controlled by one voice, one heart, one desire.

The silky honey of her lips caressed every nerve within Dan, leaving him breathless, weak with wanting.

Suddenly he cursed himself for having been a fool and not taking her to a motel. She'd probably expected it. Then he remembered the time. It was too late, now. Oh, he could get away with it, but it was too late, for too many reasons.

"When will I see you again?" Gale was asking.

They were in front of her apartment door. Somehow they'd gotten there, even though Dan couldn't remember having left the car or walking. It was like a movie cut. The whole evening had been like a series of dissolves and cuts, spinning dizzily from one place to another, without any gaps, without any bridges.

He'd forgotten to tell her all about the scene she'd done; he'd forgotten everything except the moment, the instant which had became a whole evening, over eight hours of magic.

"I will see you again?" Gale asked. There was no doubt in her eyes; only her words and voice held that emotion.

"Yes," he told her, kissing those soft, beautiful lips.

"Yes," he said, a few moments later, holding the door open. "I'll call you..."

The door closed and the romantic mood shivered away, leaving the real world, the slow, minute by minute harsh world that was his every day existence.

As he walked back to the car, Dan remembered Holly Hill, and he felt sick inside.

There would be a scene if Holly learned about his activities this evening A big bloody scene. He didn't look forward to it

While sitting in his car with the engine idling he looked up at the neat, modern apartment house. He saw the image of Gale Ross, misty, and ghost-like between him and the building, and realized anything would be worth what he had experienced with this woman, this evening. It was so special that he would never forget a wonderful moment, sensation. It was like being in love with magic. With a beautiful Goddess who simply cast a spell over every man who crossed her path. And that was silly; but what he'd experienced.

And, as somebody had told him, don't shit on your experiences.

Driving home, he tried to keep her image before his eyes; tried to think of nothing other than the pleasure they had enjoyed in each other's company.

As he climbed into bed, an hour later, Dan was still thinking about Gale Ross, but this time more intimately. He wondered what it would be like to make love to her; he wondered what it would be like to have her lying there beside him, filling his whole being with her magic.

He was still wondering several hours later when he awoke to find the mid-morning sun glaring across his eyes.

But now he wondered if it had all really happened, or had it been merely a trick of his mind. Was it all part of an illusion, a dream, and a male fantasy? Gale Ross had created so much magic in those hours that he was convinced it had to be one of the best acting performances he'd ever been exposed to.

Back to reality.

Another day, he thought, while climbing out of bed, *and another girl.*

CHAPTER FIFTEEN

Gale was tired, but happy, happier than she'd ever been as she slipped into bed. Sleep didn't really closed around her thrilling thoughts. Her mind was wrapped in the memory of Dan Blair and the evening, and was still awake when Mildred came storming into the room, all fire and anger.

Gale heard the raging outburst, hardly understanding a word Mildred said.

The other woman had been furious when she awoke in the living room to discover Gale hadn't come home early and hadn't awakened her when she had come home.

Only when the woman sat down next to her, snapped Gale's head at attention by gripping it with a delicate hand, did she pay real attention.

"I said—*you aren't listening.*" Mildred's face was contorted with both rage and passion.

"I was listening—and I'm sorry, Milly." Gale stared into the hard feminine face and felt cheap at having ever allowed anything intimate develop between them.

She gently took Mildred's hand away from her face, got up from the bed grabbed her robe, drew it around her body.

130

Mildred's eyes were burning at her.

"It's late, Milly," Gale warned, walking into the bathroom. "Don't you have to get to work?"

"What happened?" Mildred demanded, her voice calmer, more controlled. She was standing in the doorway, studying Gale. "You look as if...well, different!"

"I am different, Milly," Gale said, turning, staring impersonally into the other's eyes. "Or maybe, just back to normal. Back to my normal self."

"And what does *that* mean!" Mildred snapped, tensing, her eyes spitting fire.

Gale made up her mind. Just like that, without any conscious planning or thought.

"I'm moving out, getting a place of my own. I'm sorry, but that's the way it is."

Mildred's face drew tighter. It seemed to pale and her lush lips opened as if to say something, but just hung there, trembling.

"I'm really sorry, Milly. It was fun—but the games are over. I know it's a dirty trick to pull...but I didn't plan it this way. It happened. The mistake was letting this start in the beginning. I can't live this kind of life—I knew it would have to end someday—just didn't think it would be so soon. Maybe it should have been sooner. I'm in love—and I don't care about anything else right now but enjoying that feeling. I'm in love with a *man*—you understand, a *man!*"

Mildred seemed to find her voice then. "What'd he do, lay you...oh, come on, Gale, you can't be that serious. A man gets you all hot and bothered and you run off like a little school girl, panties burning in her hands...what's with you? Maybe you should think it over. Think it over very seriously. You can't turn me off like that, Gale. Believe me—you don't turn me off!" Her fingers snapped in Gale's face, a fraction from her nose. "Not like that, you can't!"

With that, Mildred turned, furious. She dressed noisily, slamming dresser drawers, but Gale hardly paid any attention.

She was glad when Mildred slammed the front door on her way out.

Then, and only then, Gale moved. She had a lot of packing to do; a lot of work ahead of her, and might as well start right away.

It was well past noon when Gale lifted her last luggage into the trunk of her car. A few moments later she started the engine and drove down the street.

She was humming happily all the time, and thinking about Dan Blair.

Gale drove around, looking for an apartment she could move into right away. It was late in the afternoon before she found a place that rented by the month. The landlord was pleased to rent the apartment, and Gale was glad to find it, even though the rooms were dark, gloomy, and depressing. It was a place to crash; nothing more.

By six-thirty she remembered work, and realized she was late. The unpacking hadn't even begun.

After a moment's hesitation she decided the hell with work and continued unpacking. That night she would sleep well.

By eight-thirty she was lying exhausted on the small double bed, dreaming about Dan and herself and the future.

* * * * * * *

Mildred Mason couldn't keep her mind on her work all morning. Several times she called home, but there wasn't any answer. At noon she drove to the apartment, and in a building blind rage searched the rooms and then left. A strange feeling that something was wrong, missing, plagued her all the way back to the office. She was typing when she realized what it was.

Gale's make-up was missing, the picture on the wall over the sofa was gone. Several other things had been lacking in the rooms.

Without realizing what she was doing, Mildred found herself walking out of the office. She'd told her boss something about being sick, and it was quite true. A clamping sickness was driving her stomach to the edge of convulsing inside out.

All the way back to the apartment Mildred's mind was spinning in a pit of black nausea. As she stepped into the rooms she had shared with Gale, her eyes rushed over every place that should have things of Gale's. Everything was gone.

"Gale, you can't do that!" Mildred screamed, swinging her arm across the dressing table, scattering bottles, lipstick, and powder boxes across the room, against the wall, on the floor. The rage threw her to the bed, screaming, tearing her fingers into the blankets.

"She can't...can't!" Mildred screamed, running from the bedroom, finding the phone. She had to dial three times before getting the number right.

A man's voice, which sounded more feminine

SEX QUEEN, BY CHARLES NUETZEL

than most women, said: "Franklin Agency, what can I do for you?"

"Frankie...Mildred. I want you to cut Gale Ross out...completely. I want her finished! Stopped. Dead in her bloody tracks!"

"What are you talking about?"

"That bitch has run out...that little slutting tramp is running out of my life...you gotta fix her—and good—for good. I don't care how you do it—get her fixed so she doesn't get any more parts at that bastard studio..." she raged on and on until the man's voice finally shouted for her to stop.

Her breasts were heaving, her throat dry, the vision in front of her face was blurred, as she listened to the man's words.

"Okay, honey, I'll do what I can...but she's not on contract there, and Van Houten can only cut her out of the film and see she doesn't get any more work at the studio—give her bad recommendation and—"

"I want more. You drop her! You drop her good...right on her cute little ass! You understand, Frankie?" Mildred demanded.

"Anything you say, honey. Anything."

"Just remember that I was the one who fixed you up with a real nice guy...you remember that and you—"

"How can I forget, honey? I'll do what I can. Your Gale Ross will have one hell of a job ever getting any more parts in the studios, now. Is that what you want?"

Mildred laughed cruelly. "That's exactly what I want, Frankie. I want her cut off, cold and forever! The fucking little bitch! *Exactly!*"

134

CHAPTER SIXTEEN

Dan sat in Holly's living room, waiting for the grand entrance. He had fixed himself a Scotch and soda and settled in a large, comfortable over-stuffed chair, opposite the fireplace with its huge picture of Holly Hill over it. He thought about the day, and the frustrations of wanting to shout to the world about Gale Ross. Both his personal feelings that sang through every nerve, and the professional joy at finding a real star, a real young actress who could go right to the top, first time around, thrilled through him.

Dan had tried to get in touch with Jack Davis, the producer who had talked to him some weeks ago at a party, about directing a movie. A Jack Davis would be out of his mind not to take a woman like Gale Ross for such a movie.

And
INTRODUCING...
Gale Ross

And the world would discover the great talents of a new stellar star. A lovely, beautiful nova exploding across the universe. And the movie would become a sleeper which would make more money than all the spectaculars bound together in one lump. Make Gale Ross. Make Dan Blair. A real combination; a real magic combination which would bring Hollywood to its knees before their combined talents.

It was a dream worth dreaming.

Holly Hill stood in the way, right at the present. He couldn't take much more of the demanding actress and her lusting nympho body.

Dan gulped the Scotch, got up and poured himself another, stood by the bar, leaning against it. Thinking.

If only he could get hold of Jack Davis—or even Van Houten. Anybody of authority who he could put the pressure on. The Jack Davis idea had stormed his mind when he couldn't have Van Houten at his finger tips. Murry was still in Frisco, doing God knew what!

"Hello, Darling," Holly Hill's voice exploded into being in front of him. "You're dreaming!"

She was poured into a white dress designed to squeeze around the bulging explosion of her large breasts. Holly's hips fought the battle of the middle-aged bulge with her dress. She sipped from his drink. Her eyes fastened on to his.

"I missed you, Darling. Recovered from your cold?" There was just a slight accent to her last word.

"Better, thanks."

"Where did you spend the cold? In the hospital?" she screamed, slapping the glass out of his hand. It clattered across the bar and shattered on the floor. "You dirty, two-timing shit!"

136

Her hand clawed out across his cheek. He felt the trickle of blood sting his flesh.

Dan's fist doubled up, automatically; it threatened Holly, foolishly.

"Don't you ever do that again!" he warned.

Holly laughed at his face.

"You'll hit me, Darling?" She twisted around, wiggled across the room, faced him again and sneered: "Where were you, Dan!"

For a moment he stood there, paralyzed.

"I phoned you—but dear, darling, sick Dan wasn't home." Her voice was silky sweet, spitting out hatred. Her eyes turned greener, her lips, thinned into a sneer. "I wanted you, Dan...I felt sorry for you...*I* was going to come over and comfort you— take care of you. Imagine that! Just imagine that. The Great Holly Hill, taking care of you—you, *nothing!*" Her fists slammed at her waist. Her face grew red, contorting, twisting ugly. "Me, I, Holly Hill, wanting to go over and comfort you, because you were sick. I got worried when you didn't answer the phone, so I went to your apartment...*Me,* I drove all the way out to your crummy little cheap apartment to see if I could help you...and know what I found there? Nothing, you damned bastard. Nothing! You weren't there...you weren't anywhere around. I made quite a fuss...one of your neighbors got all excited, came out to find what was making the noise." Her lip grinned, spreading wide, her eyes danced. "He liked what he found. Was he surprised to find the Holly Hill...big Hollywood star...standing there. He was nice. Said you'd gone out, and offered me a drink. We had several."

"So what's the complaint?" Dan knew the man

137

would be Ralph Larson, an insurance agent, a good guy, and quite a man with the women. Holly would like a man like Ralph. "Didn't you enjoy yourself?"

"Hell, no," she spat out, lunging across the room, slamming her hands down on the bar, leaning toward him, her face stopping only an inch away. "Hell, no! And you know why? Because he didn't rate...he was a dud—a real dud."

"Ralph?"

"A dud, Dan. A real dud!" She laughed at his face. "Talked up a storm with you? Well, take it from me he can't make any more of a point than a...little boy. I threw myself at him—and he ran away until I had him trapped!" Holly laughed, pushing her face closer to his. "I tried! But he's nothing like you—nothing like you at all!" For a long moment she stood there, her lips only a breath from his, her eyes searching, the anger slowly lifting and disappearing

"Nobody's like you, Dan!" she finally said in a small voice

Dan just stood there, stunned speechless

The sudden change numbed him. And what she said added to the numbness both about himself and Ralph. But mostly about himself.

She wasn't getting seriously? That was all he needed

"Where were you, Dan?" she asked in a meek voice, stepping away, staring at him, her face tortured with emotion that hadn't been there before. Her large eyes seemed misty, on the verge of breaking into tears.

"Where were you?" she repeated in a shaking voice.

138

SEX QUEEN, BY CHARLES NUETZEL

Suddenly Dan felt sorry for her. She was just a woman, after all, a woman who desperately wanted love and didn't know how to get it. At least not the kind of love she so badly craved.

He wondered if she would have been happier if Elliott Wood had somehow managed to marry her, to convince her that a career wasn't worth the price she would have to pay. He wondered if she ever thought of Elliott, and realized the mistake she'd made some twenty years before.

"Look, Holly," he said in a tender voice, "this is all wrong. You surely know that...we can't keep up this little game...it's just hurting you and—"

"Shut up! I don't want to hear it...I don't want to hear anything!" Then she was in his arms. "Just love me, Dan. Love me, and don't let me think...don't let me think about anything, about anything at all. Only in your arms can I stop thinking..."

It all sounded like scripted lines from a hack, B movie.

What kind of foolish lies was she feeding her sad mind? What silly illusions made her say such things?

Dan didn't want to kiss her, he didn't want to make love to her; but he couldn't say that to Holly.

Her lips quivered against his, her tongue pressed against his teeth, greedily trying to find an opening into which to plunge. When he gave it to her, she tensed against him as if life depended on what was happening.

Her breasts cushioned against his chest, her tongue danced deep into his mouth, thrusting in and out, and she wrapped her arms around his neck, as only a desperate woman would do.

139

"Love me, Dan...oh, dear, God, please love me," she pleaded, as they broke the kiss. She kept clinging against him. Her whole frame was trembling, sobs sounding past her lips. "Love me...please, just love me..."

"Take it easy," he said, gently. "You need a drink…"

"Maybe...maybe."

Dan mixed stiff drinks of Scotch for both of them, handed her one and gulped from his own glass. They watched each other across the bar. She poured herself a second Scotch and then a third. On the fourth she waited, looking at the amber liquor in the glass, clutching it tight in her hands.

"You know, Darling," she finally said, looking up into his eyes, "I should hate you..."

"Let's not talk."

She nodded, looked down at the glass again and then tipped it to her lips. The Scotch disappeared. She slammed the glass on the bar, gripped hold of his hand, and said: "Come on, lover...let's get this over with!"

They left the living room, walked up the stairs, and found her bedroom without a word.

She closed the door behind them, then turned, looking at him.

"I *am* beautiful, aren't I, Darling?" She stood there, leaning back against the door, challenging him with her eyes. It was a standard dramatic pose she had used in many movies.

"Yes, you're beautiful, Holly."

"A man would really want me, wouldn't he? I mean, I'm still desirable? I haven't changed that much. And men, all over the world want their illu-

140

SEX QUEEN, BY CHARLES NUETZEL

sion of what I am. And I am that. Aren't I?"

He said what she wanted to hear. Then Holly walked over to him, turned, said: "Unzip me, lover."

Dan automatically unzipped the dress that fell in a pool around her feet. She leaned back against him, gripped his hands, pressing them into her large, supple breasts.

"I love you, Dan. Really, love you," she breathed in a husky voice.

He didn't say anything, instead, kissed her neck, worried her ear with his lips and tongue. It was what she wanted; what she needed. He felt sorry enough for Holly to do this much. She seemed different tonight, or was he really seeing her for the pitiful thing she was?

There would never be enough love to fill the void in her needy soul.

She pressed against him, her throat murmured under his lips, her body seemed strangely relaxed, almost childlike.

"Love me, Darling," she murmured softly, suddenly turning in his arms, her lips finding his, blindly.

The kiss was gentle, the first gentle kiss he had experienced with Holly Hill. Every night, so far, in her Beverly Hills house was like the first time, savage, wild, cruel.

"Love *me,* Dan," she whispered again, tensing, straining, her lips suddenly biting into his, her teeth grinding, hurting, and bruising.

Then she whipped away, her eyes flashing lustfully into his.

"Help me," she demanded, gripping his arms. "Take off the bra."

He hugged her to him, unclasped the bra, and pulled it around her body until it fell free of her breasts.

Those large orbs of flesh hung there before him, soft, yielding, eager, hot.

The mere physical need, the hunger which had plagued him all day as an aftermath of not having taken Gale Ross to a motel, not wanting to have ruined the perfection of their first date together, surged up through Dan, and he pulled Holly roughly into his arms, the way she liked it, the way he suddenly needed it. It was going to be savage taking, releasing, a sexual exchange of two desperate animals releasing their raw needs, and nothing more.

All the hate and anger at the world, at the human race, bubbled over Dan and he ground his mouth against Holly's, plunged his tongue deep into the open offering of her trembling lips. Her breasts clung to his clothing, her lips twisted against his hips, bringing the need stronger within him.

They broke away, hurried to the bed, and after Holly had clawed his clothing from him they embraced each other. Their bodies joined without any preliminaries. There wasn't any need to wait. Holly needed him desperately and her hunger had fired the basic animal spark within him.

As their hips thrust together; as their bodies became one raging fire of movement, Dan felt an explosive blast of need bursting out of him in one surging release. At the same time the woman gulped out erotic sounds that drove her tighter against him. Her hands clawed deep into the muscles of his back in the last hectic moments of their physical need. It was nothing but a savage lusting of two animals ramming at one another in a selfish bestial need.

"I love you, Dan...love you..." she murmured over and over in his ears.

It was difficult to tell if those words were well rehearsed statements, lines from a script, or real feelings the woman was expressing. It was unsettling and even a bit frightening to him.

For a long time they clung to each other, bathed in sweat, exhausted to the edge of sleep. Dan wasn't really sure if sleep hadn't embraced his mind or not. He simply became aware of Holly's erotic movements which sprang a reaction into his nerves.

"Love me, Dan?" she asked, clinging to him.

"No," he said, startled by his own word.

She froze, like hard stone, stared at him. "Why?"

That one question was so anguished, so heart rending, that Dan was sorry for having told her the brutal truth. There wasn't anything but to continue, as honestly as before.

"I'm sorry, Holly. You're a wonderfully desirable woman. A man...couldn't possibly help desiring you—but..." He shrugged. "It wasn't meant for us.... You surely know..."

"I *don't* know!" she yelled, sitting up. Her face wrinkled in pain, her eyes moist, her lush lips parted, gasped in air, causing the huge swells of her breasts to heave up and down. "What's wrong... wrong with me...that...a man...?"

"Nothing, Holly—that has nothing to do with it."

"What does it have to do with, then?" she fairly screamed at him. Again it was difficult to tell if this was the real Holly or something fashioned out of some lost, but suddenly remembered, script.

"Men have loved you."

"Sure many, I know that. But I want you!"

"What's so special about me?" he countered. "I'm just here, that's all. Is that it?"

"Oh, for God's sake!" she spat out. Then suddenly she covered her face with trembling hands. "You don't know how difficult..." The words faded. "What's wrong with wanting to be loved?"

The anguish in those words convinced him this was the real Holly. The one which Elliott had begged him to be caring about. And had told him about.

"All I've wanted," she muttered into her hands, "is to be loved, not used. Not just an object. Yet...that's what I've become. I know that. An image on the screen that all men are supposed to love, desire. And it is difficult to live up to that." She pulled her hand away from her face, wiped tears from her eyes, then looked at him, almost pleading. "Can't you just love me, why can't you? What's wrong?"

She seemed like a little child, desperate. For the moment he was looking into the real Holly. And her words weren't about him so much as they were about the need for a man to consider her special in a personal way. For a moment she was stripped naked in front of him, emotionally raw, stark and blatantly honest.

"Quite frankly, I'm not any different from any other woman...that image of me on the screen, and what I play out so many times here in real life—that's all a terrible, perverse act, a cartoon concerning a thing that doesn't really even exist. I sometimes wonder if I exist at all! Has anybody ever loved me? Really loved me as a person? Or is it all a fake?"

He gazed tenderly at her, suddenly feeling a totally different emotional reaction towards the woman, the human under the very erotic image. "I know that Elliott Wood loved you and—"

He broke off at the sudden outburst that convulsed Holly's body into unexpected action.

She recoiled from him as if bodily slapped. She started to say something, then her lips shut. Her whole body went rigid, then crumbled. Tears welled in her eyes, then she flung herself on the bed, sobbing, soft anguished sounds breaking from her lips. For a long time she was totally lost in her own emotional outburst.

For only a moment it was like some scene in one of her films, and then he realized that in no way was this an act. She had been surprised by the mention of Elliott's name.

Tenderly, Dan touched her, but she pushed him away, angrily.

"Holly," he said softly. "Come on...please."

"Don't!" she whispered so softly that he almost didn't hear the word. The woman froze, was silent, breathing more evening, then suddenly she sat up, her cheeks wet with tears, the make-up around her eyes already following the tears.

"Silly me!" she stated, as if embarrassed. Then just as suddenly, lips trembling slightly, she asked: "How...how is...Elliott? We had such a nice thing so many years ago. I hope he's found some peace, happiness. He deserves it."

"Fine...he's pretty serious with my secretary,"

he told her, trying to smile.

Her face worked together into a twisted expression of agony. "We...were...serious...you know. I loved him—but...I loved acting more...a nasty reality which has been very expensive in so many ways. A girl, anybody, can become obsessed... and it has to be that way, or you don't get anywhere in this business. There is no real room for emotional tangles if you want to really make it big. At least not for a woman like me. I had to be free to play it hard ball with any person, no matter what. And, quite frankly, it cost me. I had to lose him. But it was a wonderful experience. We were young and very much in love."

"I know—he told me."

"I've...never known a man...like him," she whispered to herself. Then, as if not conscious that he had heard her, she said: "I hate all that. Too much pain! Damn Elliott, anyway!"

Suddenly Holly's face hardened, her eyes glazed over for a moment, looking at the wall behind him, then slowly they shifted, focusing on Dan. A shifting of moods flashed across her face, as if differing pictures were being run through her brain. Then, without warning, Holly reached for him.

"Make love to me!" she demanded. "That's what I want. That's all I want. I don't like this conversation. I don't like talking. I want you to just make me forget it all. Let's just be very real sexy to one another. Here...make love to them!" She cupped her breasts, offering them to him, the nipples already rigid. "Start here...and just devour me alive! Make me forget all this crap!"

The shifting moods had wrapped around him,

146

from tenderness to pure erotic need. This woman, regardless of anything else, was sex in the raw.

And they moved together.

No words, no tenderness; just two savage animals, crushing against each other. Her fingers gripped deep against his own, the nails attempting to cut the flesh as she pulled him into her arms. By then Dan didn't care much about anything. Holly was in command, acting or offering real passion didn't matter. Her body just wrapped itself around him, demandingly.

But in the final moments, as their bodies lurched together, as her hips pressed to Dan she sobbed, low, soft in his ear, words of love, words that didn't have any clear form, until he heard a name, a name which sent a chill down his spine and brought him back to the sane, civilized world. The jungle of passion tore away, sliced by sharp razors. He was aware of that name ringing over and over again in his ears, hardly aware of the fire which suddenly burst free from him, uniting them in one final, last moment of passion.

Afterwards, Dan moved from Holly.

She stood there, her face blank, her lips trembling, her eyes focused on infinity. She had heard the words, too, she had heard the name that rang out from some deep well of her need. And that one name had defeated her.

Dan left Holly there, just staring into infinity, knowing instinctively that she would want to be alone.

He found his clothes, dressed, walked out of the house he would never have to enter again. He knew too much about Holly; he knew what she hadn't wanted to admit to herself; a truth that would make his presence too painful.

Somehow he felt sorry, terribly sorry for Holly Hill, and wished there was some way he could help. No one could really help Holly; nothing could really give her escape from the hell her life had become. Only one person could possibly have helped, some time in the distant past, but it was too late for that, too.

She had called out the man's name in an anguish of passion, need, and pain.

Holly was alone in her fame, alone in her agony, alone in a world which loved her image, but where nobody, not a single soul loved the woman who lived in that lush body.

Dan felt sorry for Holly and shivered at the desires which could drive a woman to make herself into a Holly Hill.

CHAPTER SEVENTEEN

Dan had seen the headlines, HOLLYWOOD QUEEN FOUND DEAD. He didn't need to know what Queen it was.

The headlines were different, but they all said the same thing:

Holly Hill killed herself some time in the morning; she was found, by her butler dead in her swimming pool.

Dan had arrived late in the morning at the studio.

Everything lacked reality. He was dazed, as if viewing everything through a fog. He was emotionally detached. And somehow it didn't surprise him. Nor did he, at first, feel much more than a sadness for Holly. It all seemed just too logical; too tragic. When he drove into the parking lot the place was crowded with reporters. He was stopped a dozen times on his way to the office.

By then Dan was numbed, unable to speak when he stopped in front of Doris Patton's desk.

"Van Houten wants you!" she announced in an even voice. She wasn't screaming, but his head was, and the whole world was screaming.

WHY?

Dan knew why, but he didn't understand. He just couldn't focus on anything other than the inner pain that Holly's death caused in him. It wasn't as if a dear friend had died, but rather a sense of anguish over a sad person's death, somebody one knew about, yet didn't have any real emotional attachments to. Even if he'd been a part of her last days—that had been a forced thing; any feelings for the woman herself were a matter of that last hour together—and that was terribly mixed and confused.

"Where's Elliott?"

"He was in...a moment ago—he looked *white.*" Doris' eyes misted. "He loved her once, you know."

"Yes. Where's Murry?"

"In his office. I'll call and tell him you're on your way."

"No—wait. Have a copy of the paper?"

Doris nodded, gave him the Morning Times. The headlines were bold, black:

HOLLY FOUND DEAD IN POOL!

Slamming the door behind him, Dan walked around his desk, and sat down. His eyes were still hypnotized by the banner headline. This was like a nightmare. Reality was ramming in on his brain. Now he could feel the pain. It didn't seem possible. It couldn't be possible. Yet, he should have guessed. What a damned fool he'd been leaving her there; leaving her alone.

He turned to the article under the huge picture of Holly that covered half the front page.

The paper gave the bare details. Holly had been found floating head down in the large pool, by her

150

butler. He had called the police. The studio would make no statement. The police were investigating, but there was no doubt that she'd killed herself. A note had been found. The contents hadn't been revealed to the newspapers. Mr. Morris Van Houten, president of *Van Houten Pictures, Inc.* had examined the note, but refused comment. The rest of the long article told about Holly's climb to fame, listed some of her most famous roles and her last film, which hadn't been released.

Doris stepped into the room, handed him a paper cup.

"This will help," she said.

"Thanks." It was whiskey. The liquor burned, but he didn't notice. A lump was caught in his throat and moisture clouded his vision.

Damned Holly! he cursed silently to himself. *What a damned fool thing to do.*

"Where's Elliott?"

"I don't know."

"Get him—I want to see him."

Dan kept staring at the paper, but not seeing it. He kept seeing the picture of Holly, her eyes staring blindly, her whole body sagging, defeated. What had she been thinking? What could she have been thinking?

Hell, if she'd only waited until she was sober, until she could think straight. It hadn't been worth it. Holly Hill had everything except the one thing she missed completely out on: real love.

Love makes the world go round and round and round, dizzily; the lack of it had made Holly's stop cold: and she had killed herself.

Why couldn't she have been content with what

she'd won out of life? Why couldn't she simply face the truth, and enjoyed her fame, her glory, and her money. Hell, she'd been able to force him into a command love affair—and she could get any man she wanted, either by throwing herself at the guy, or by pressuring him. And maybe that's exactly what she didn't want. Wasn't that what she was telling him in so many ways?

Life was difficult to survive; some made it, other's just gave up or were crushed by events beyond their control. Those that managed to avoid the killing forces thrashing in and around them had to pay a price, too. Age had frightened Holly. And had defeated her.

Holly wanted love. How she'd wanted and needed love last night, Dan thought, looking at the empty paper cup in his hand.

He needed another drink.

The door burst open and a raging cannon ball of human fury slammed a fist on Dan's desk.

Murry Van Houten glared down at him.

"Why aren't you in my office?" he cried, but his voice didn't have the solid strength to sound anything other than tired. Totally defeated.

"What can I do—now?" Dan inquired, emotionally drained. He wanted to go away and get drunk.

"Explain this!" Van Houten slammed down a piece of paper.

"What is it?" Dan didn't look, he was afraid to look.

"Read the thing, damn you—and explain!" The man's eyes looked tired, his lips weren't even hard anymore. Van Houten looked too exhausted to even fight. He was a tired old man who had suffered a

152

complete personal and business loss. It was a toss-up as to which hurt more.

Dan slowly took the piece of paper, guessing what it was. Somehow Murry had gotten Holly's suicide note.

The words were written in a tight, neat little rhythm. He wondered how hard Holly had worked on it; how long she had taken to put her last agony on paper:

> *"To Whom it May Concern:*
>
> *"I don't see any need to continue. I want to die because there isn't anything left for me to live for. I know now what has moved me throughout my life, and I can't live with that knowledge. Maybe somebody will understand and forgive. Maybe in death I will find what I couldn't get in life.*
>
> *Ann Hill."*

Dan hadn't even known her real name. He wondered what the Ann that Elliott had known was like. Maybe a little like what he'd seen for a brief moment the night before, perhaps like the woman who had reached him and touched him, and created a tenderness, a momentary understanding. Only Elliott would know.

Dan had to find Elliott. He had to get rid of Van Houten.

"What about it?" Dan asked, looking up at the studio boss, trying not to reveal any outward emotion.

"You tell *me!* What did she mean?"

"Oh, come on, Murry, I wasn't her father confessor! Hell, you know all about that! What is there to make of it?" Dan stood, shrugged.

Morris Van Houten stared probingly at Dan, as if trying to read into his mind. Then the large shoulders sagged. "Damned, she was an expensive product and I want to know what killed her."

"She killed herself," Dan announced.

"Funny! If I find out you had anything to do with this, I'll have your job, funny man—just remember that! I'll have your job, but fast! You just remember that, Sweetheart!" With that, Morris Van Houten slouched out of the room, slamming the door behind him.

Dan stood there, undecided as to what to do. Then he leaned over the desk, pressed the Intercom. "Find Elliott?"

Doris' voice answered him: "No...but I think I know where you can—at the *Stage Bar.*"

"Call, find out if he's there. If he is, tell him to wait, I have to see him. Elliott will understand."

Dan waited. Eternity passed. He heard Doris' voice announce that Elliott was at the *Stage Bar* and would wait.

Dan rushed out of the office, then off the lot. Five minutes later he stepped into the dimly lit cocktail lounge. For a moment he had trouble finding Elliott. The man was hunched over the bar, a drink in his hand.

Dan pulled on Elliott's arm. "Over there," he said, pointing to a corner booth. Then to the bartender: "A couple of rounds of what he's having—

for both of us!"

They sat in the dimness of the small booth, opposite each other. A twenty-year lover, a modern counterpart, the male stud, both of which had helped to drive Holly into her pool grave.

They both had tragic faces, drawn, and pale. Neither looked at the other.

Dan waited for his drink, gulped the first and fingered the second. The Scotch burned, settled and crept into Dan's brain. He waited it out until brain and booze mixed.

"Elliott...I'm sorry."

The writer shrugged. "Shouldn't mean anything to me."

"I thought you might want to know she still loved you."

Elliott's eyes snapped up to Dan's. "What?"

"She loved you."

A groan murmured deep in the Elliott's chest, caught in his throat and then sighed softly out past tight lips. Elliott gulped the two Scotches.

"I didn't love her any more, Dan," he said.

"I know."

"Believe me...Doris and I are getting married in a few months, you know."

"No, I didn't." Dan felt the surprise, and the relief. If Elliott was going to marry another woman, then there wasn't any reason not to tell the rest. "It happened last night, Elliott. At a moment which, well...when she didn't have a chance to think what she was saying. She called out your name..."

Elliott's face showed no reaction. Only his eyes seemed to respond to the words. After a moment he snapped his fingers at the bartender, ordered another round for them and said to Dan: "Funny, a few years ago I would have given my right arm to hear that...maybe even a few months ago—who knows. I feel sorry for Holly. She ruined her own life—and damaged a lot of others. The public will never know—and maybe that's good. We had something, Dan, something pretty good, but it was her choice between a career or marriage. She made her own choice. She couldn't blend both. It was a one-way deal with her. Well...I don't know." He shrugged as the new round of drinks was placed in front of them.

They sat there for a long time, each trapped in his own thoughts, and then suddenly the mood lifted slightly.

Holly was part of the past for both of them. Each in his own way would be haunted by the memory of Holly Hill, actress, woman, and lover.

Elliott smiled for the first time. "Hell, man, I just told you I was going to get married!"

"Why didn't Doris tell me?"

"I told her to save that for me! I wanted the pleasure. She can tell her girl friends!" He laughed; and even though it sounded slightly forced, it had an honest ring to it. "She's a wonderful woman. Make a good mother. I love her, Dan—and I guess she loves me that's what she did say, anyway, and that's what every guy wants. A girl who loves him."

Dan saluted with his Scotch, and thought silently to himself: *and every woman, even a Holly Hill. And especially Ann Hill.*

CHAPTER EIGHTEEN

Dan was drunk as hell as he looked at the door. It was where life had become reality for him, it was where he had lost paradise.

Knocking on the door, pounding on it, Dan called out her name.

"Gale—are you there—Gale!"

The door suddenly swung open.

The woman called Mildred Mason looked out.

"Gale doesn't live here any more—*well*, if it isn't Mr. Dan Blair!" The face leered at him for a moment and then after hesitating, the woman said:

"What'd you do to her?"

Dan tried to figure out what the woman meant. It seemed as if this Mildred Mason was glaring at him with hate in her eyes; or was it invitation? He didn't know. Nor care.

"Mind if I come in?" he asked, pushing his way into the apartment. He pressed accidentally against the hefty thrust of the woman's breast. Slamming the door closed with his foot, Dan found himself suddenly embracing this Mildred Mason. It was automatic, without any real thought. He was dazed in his own emotional confusion. She was a woman, and he was drunk. And hurting. And he didn't care.

157

Mildred struggled in his arms, and for a moment Dan was confused, wondering if Holly had come back from the dead to plague him.

"Let go of me, you ape!" she cried, pressing her hands against his chest.

Dazed, Dan stepped back, against the door.

She laughed. "Sorry. I'm not interested! Thanks. But no thanks. Especially you—or any other man!" Realizing she'd said too much, Mildred spat out, "Get out of my apartment. I don't want your kind around. I have my own...man!"

Puzzled, Dan left the apartment. The whole scene was pure insanity. Why he'd made a stumbling pass at the woman he had no idea. He not only didn't know her, he wasn't even interested. He sat in his car, the night dark around him, thinking. The first thought was he needed another drink. The second was remembering where Gale worked. Then he was there, in the cocktail lounge. A tall, slender woman leaned over his table, smiled, said: "Hi! How're you?"

He looked up. Loreen something, he remembered. "Where's Gale?"

"She doesn't work here any more," Loreen the waitress told him in a sultry voice. Her eyes flirted, the left winked. "But I'm willing for a second round."

"Give me a Martini—No!...I'd better stick to Scotch!" The woman left, returned. Returned a second and a third time. He finished each drink, slow and easy. The evening seemed to slip away. He sat there, silently listening to the music in the background; trying to ignore the rage of his thoughts.

Dan hadn't returned to the studio that day. He

158

had stayed at the *Stage Bar,* with Elliott. Things had blurred and he'd found himself standing in front of the door which had once belonged to a beautiful young woman with golden hair and sky blue eyes.

Loreen sat down next to him. Her thigh pressed his. "Ready to go, lover?"

He looked at her. "Where?"

The liquor was buzzing bees in his head. The room was contorting, growing both large and small all at the same time.

"Anywhere lover!" she invited.

Somehow Dan managed to wade through the reasoning necessary to understand what she had said.

He stood and the room stood with him.

"Hey, watch out, lover," Loreen's voice warned, as she gripped his arm. "You need *coffee.*"

"I need...what *I* need," he said, controlling his voice, forcing the room to behave itself. He turned, studied Loreen's features and grinned. "Come on, baby, let's go someplace."

"You sure?"

"Sure!"

He grabbed hold of her arm and she propelled him across the cocktail lounge. Finding his car was a little harder. But he found it.

Why the woman was driving, Dan couldn't understand at first. He couldn't remember getting into the car. He couldn't remember anything except finding it.

She parked the car in front of his apartment, helped him out and helped him upstairs. She opened the door and urged him in.

For a moment Dan swayed, standing in the middle of his living room. Then, as Loreen came up to him, tried to get hold of his arm, Dan swung her around, covered her lips with kisses.

She struggled only for a second and then pressed eagerly against him.

"Hey—you still got some fire left!" she cried, grinning, her eyes happy fires.

"Damned right!" Dan grabbed the woman, took her into the bedroom and found the bed, blindly.

They fell down, tangled on the bed, surged together.

His hand searched up her skirt, caressed over nylon, touched warm flesh and leaped upwards.

The woman squealed, trapped his fingers with her thighs, laughed and bit his mouth with moist lips, deep kissing for a long time.

Somehow he'd managed to get her skirt up over her hips, but couldn't remember having done so. He sat over her, looking down, trying unsuccessfully to focus his eyes.

Then blackness fluttered, vision disappeared.

The blackness reshaped itself.

He was looking into darkness, up at the ink ceiling. He heard breathing next to him. Wondering who it was, Dan turned and saw the naked female lying there on the bed.

For a moment he didn't remember who she was; then vaguely the events of the evening took shape.

He had wanted Gale Ross and had ended with this woman.

With a groan, Dan realized he was naked. Everything seemed distant, blurred, buzzing out of focus.

The next thing Dan knew he was lying on his

back with the sun in his eyes. His head was throbbing painfully. His throat was as dry as if all the deserts in the world had been crammed between his teeth.

He heard a moan and recognized it as his own.

Moving was a problem. He didn't want to face that problem. For a long time he lay there, trying to not think about the hammers attempting to shatter his skull from the inside.

He thought about Gale. He thought about Holly and suddenly thought about Gale living Holly's life.

The thought sickened Dan.

And the problem of moving was automatically solved for him.

He doubled up. Sickness flushed from his stomach, up out of his mouth. The sickness thundered within his skull, ripped his stomach apart and then finally ebbed slowly, painfully away, leaving him whole, but agonized.

An arm circled his shoulders.

"Hey, there," a feminine voice said in concern. "Sick?"

Dan opened his eyes, realizing who was there with him, and shuddered at the thought of Loreen being in his bedroom.

"What you think!" he snapped, pushing away from the woman. He dived for the bathroom and made it just in time.

Later, Dan returned to the bedroom.

Loreen had cleaned up the mess, somehow found some new covers, and changed the bed. She sat on the edge, waiting for him.

As he stepped from the bathroom, Loreen squealed, came into his arms before he had a chance to stop her.

What the hell? he thought, holding the woman closer. He didn't need to think, not right then. He didn't want to think about anything for a while. One girl was as good as the next.

A moment later, Dan gently moved the girl to arms length.

"I need a drink, first!" he announced.

She laughed happily, followed him into the living room, to the bar, and helped herself to a stiff whiskey, which she downed in a short series of gulps

He took his drink a little slower, but not much slower. Refilling both their glasses, Dan led the way into the bedroom again.

He thought about Gale for a brief moment before folding Loreen's body against his.

Just another female to use; nothing more!

Then the thought faded, because he didn't want to think about a girl he'd never possessed, didn't know how to get in touch with, and who wasn't anywhere near at the moment.

He didn't like to think of that, at all.

Suddenly he could almost understand how Holly...no Ann...Hill must have so desperately wanted escape from the world that had become such a harsh reality to her. His had become a hellish, empty pit into which a woman like this Loreen was simply a tool to use in order to escape cold truth.

For a rest of the day Dan didn't think about anything. Because of that he managed to use Loreen Asher as he had made use of so many women on his "casting couch"—using them like toys. Like Holly Hill had used him.

162

CHAPTER NINETEEN

It was the next morning, when Dan walked into the *Van Houten Studios,* that he got his first jolt.

Doris was packing his personal possessions, hers were already gathered together. When he stepped into the office, she looked up, her face tragic.

"I'm sorry, Dan," she managed, her voice choked with emotion.

"What's happening?"

"Van Houten...he...fired you!" A sob broke her lips into a light tremble.

"What! Why?" Dan just stood there, numb, unable to believe what had happened.

"The Hill thing...he's learned you were with Holly that night—and...well, he thinks you must have had something to do with what happened."

Dan shook his head, not quite sure this was happening to him. The world had suddenly shattered, broken up into little bits.

"He fired you, too?" Dan asked, looking into the outer office where her purse and a small box were sitting in view.

Doris smiled. "I quit."

"You can't do that—"

"Elliott has asked me to marry him, you know...well, we just moved the date up a bit. I quit...he quit, too—has a job at another studio, for more money." She smiled, then stepped over and patted him on the cheek. "Poor Dan...where will you go, now?"

"To Van Houten's office and give him a piece of my mind!" But Dan didn't move. He just stared down at his secretary, who wasn't his secretary any more. "I'll miss you, Doris.

"What'll you do?" Her face showed concern. Her features appeared white against her chestnut brown hair.

"Oh, I have enough money for a short spree. There are other jobs..."

Doris was suddenly crying, tears were running down her cheeks. Her head shook from side to side. "No...oh...Dan, that bastard has put out the...word on you. Nobody in the Industry will hire you!"

Dan took her statement without any emotional reaction. He merely thought: *Of course, Murry would do that!*

He remembered Jack Davis, remembered the short film of Gale Ross that had been cut from the show, which Dave Kroph had hidden out of sight.

"All's not lost, Doris...believe me!" He wiped the tears from her cheeks with gentle fingers. "Stop all that emotional stuff, you're supposed to be happy—getting married! Elliott's a great guy."

"I know..." Her voice was still choked.

"You do me one favor?" Dan asked.

"Anything."

"Get Dave Kroph on the phone, right away."

Doris moved, went into the other room, picked

SEX QUEEN, BY CHARLES NUETZEL

up a phone and in a few seconds said: "He's on the line."

Dan grabbed the receiver on his desk.

"Dave, can you come over to my office, in a hurry? Bring that film clip on Gale Ross."

"That's Studio property, Dan...I'm sorry...I can't give you that!" Dave's voice said.

"Hell, I don't give a damned about that, Dave! Has Murry seen it, yet?"

"No...."

"Well, be a sport...give a guy a break—give a girl a break! I'll do you a favor sometime, Dave."

There was a long hesitation, then Dave's voice sighed through the receiver. "Okay, sweetheart, but just remember...oh, hell—what difference does it make, anyway. Look, I'll be over in a few minutes. Okay?"

"Fine."

Dan hung the receiver back on the hook.

Doris questioned him with her eyes. "What's this all about?"

'Something that I'll let you know all about... later. When I can. Are you quitting...work, completely?"

"Long enough to get married—maybe...if you need a good secretary, I think Elliott wouldn't mind—but...where would you...?"

"Work?" Dan shrugged. "I have to see a man about a picture, first—then I'll tell you." He grinned. "Cheer up, I have a few aces in the hole, and thank God they're still there!"

He thought for a moment, then asked: "Did Gale Ross call in to give you her new address?"

Doris frowned. "Somebody called...yesterday,

but in the hurry—yes, I think it was Miss Ross. Where the hell did I put the memo." She hurriedly looked through the papers in the waste basket.

Dan held his breath. He had to know where to get hold of Gale Ross, for more than professional reasons, even though that was enough motive. His career, any career he might ever have, would hinge on conning Jack Davis, producer of cheap quickies, into letting him direct a picture with Gale Ross starring. With a find like Gale, he'd be able to name his own meal ticket.

Dave Kroph stepped into the office, carrying a can of film.

"If Murry ever finds out about this, sweetheart, it's my neck." The man grinned, warmly. "I hope...well, I guess you have something planned— and I hope it works out. A nasty break, Dan."

He handed over the film can.

Doris stood, beaming. "Found it, Dan."

"What?"

"The address, and there's a phone number. Want me to call her?"

Dan shook his head. She gave him a crumpled slip of paper and he looked at it, studying the address, locating its position in Hollywood.

"Thanks, both of you," Dan said, starting out of the office.

"Aren't you going to see Murry?" Doris asked.

But he didn't really hear the words; Dan was already in a dream world of his own.

Once in his apartment, Dan went to the phone, and called Jack Davis' office in Beverly Hills. A secretary put him through.

"Hello, Dan baby. How are things?" Jack Davis

166

said in the receiver.

"Fine, I've come up with something you might be interested in, Jack, I think it might be worth your while to take a look at a screen test...somebody to star in one of your quickies...you know we were talking about doing something in the near future and—"

"Sorry, Dan baby, but I'm afraid things have tightened up right now...."

Dan didn't hear the rest. His ears rang with the words, but their sounds had no meaning.

Of course, the word would have reached even a man like Davis. As far as Hollywood was concerned, Dan was finished.

Dan fixed himself a drink, gulped it down and stared out his window across the late morning town spread out below. A beautiful setting for a glamour life which he'd lived for ten long years, ten years of running around, chasing his tail, like a mad dog in heat.

Then he remembered the image of Holy Hill, her face a complete blank. Such a lovely woman, if only she'd known the truth; if only she'd accepted herself for what she was.

He poured another shot of whiskey into the glass and then raised it to his lips.

To hell with the world and everything in it!

Murry would cool down, some time in the future. Murry Van Houten would cool down and realize what a bastard thing he was doing—for nothing! He *had* to!

What did the future hold? Dan wondered.

Then he remembered a magic moment, a beautiful face, upturned under his; her soft warm lips, the sigh of ocean waves whispering in the background, the delicate glow of moonlight flooding over the world, casting romantic magic over everything it touched. He remembered the love that had ebbed up through his whole being, a love which had never touched him before. And suddenly he needed to feel again. He needed something other than the mere sexual escape which had become a habit over the last years.

He thought of Gale Ross, and thought of love, and knew he would have to see her again.

After a third whiskey, Dan knew he couldn't wait to see her.

It had to be now.

CHAPTER TWENTY

It had been a surprise to learn that the *Chambers Steak House* had decided to do without her, but Gale had shook it off, called the *Van Houten Studios,* left her address and phone number with Dan Blair's office and then waited.

That night she had learned about Holly Hill's death; read the newspapers, then fell asleep late in the evening. The next morning, Gale had gotten up at eleven, dressed and faced the fact that she didn't have a job, nor enough money to get by on for more than a couple of weeks.

Dressed in a blue sheath, Gale walked out of the apartment and found her car on the street. As she started the engine, she looked up in time to see another car stop along side hers.

A man leaned out the window, grinning.

"Hi, Gale," Dan Blair said. "Need a lift?"

For a flustered moment she didn't know what to do. *What was he doing there? What did he want?*

"Where're you going?" he asked. "Any place special?"

Gale hesitated only a moment, then said: "Was going to look for a job."

"Come on...get in," was his only comment. He

169

leaned across the car, opened the other door.

She killed the engine, slipped from behind the driver's seat, and got into Dan's car.

Dan drove down the street, not saying anything until they came to Hollywood Boulevard.

"You really want to look for a job?" he asked.

"I should..."

"I thought we could go for a ride...maybe have dinner...and let things work out. How about it?" he offered.

She heard her voice, from a distance, say: "I'd love to."

They sat there staring at each other for a long time until a car behind them blasted its horn.

Dan drove across the street, found a place where he could U-turn, re-crossed Hollywood Boulevard and headed for the freeway.

She lighted a cigarette, while trying to control her shaking fingers. She was nervous, and excited. A warm glow worked over her whole body. She looked at the man and felt an emotional throb tightened deep inside her.

"You're beautiful, Gale," Dan said as they glided onto the Hollywood Freeway driving north. "Every time I see you, you look more and more beautiful."

"Thanks," was all she could trust her voice to say. Sitting there beside the man, Gale kept feeling a thrilling awareness of something stronger than casual interest. Here was a man of position, a man of Hollywood, who actually seemed to like her. Oh, she didn't fool herself into thinking he could really care one hell about her for anything more than a long night's outing. What she had felt that evening with Dan, when he had held her in his arms, couldn't have been experienced by him, as well. Gale realized she would do anything he asked. Anything at all; and was puzzled, while at the same time excited, by the calm, casual acceptance.

He was the only man, since Wayne Gilman, that Gale had been so attracted to. In fact, Wayne seemed only a thin shadow of her dead past. She had thought about nothing other than Dan Blair since going out with him.

They drove for a long time, until it was late afternoon. The San Fernando Valley gave way to mountains. The mountains gave way to desert. Neither of them said much. There really wasn't much to be said. Gale had asked about Holly Hill, but Dan refused to talk about work, and that satisfied her. Whatever Dan wanted.

It was getting dark. The sun dipped over the edge of the earth in a spray of orange red, lighting the desert world in streaks of vivid color.

Dan continued to drive in silence.

Hunger gnawed at Gale's stomach and she lighted her last cigarette.

"When do we eat?" she asked.

Dan nodded, said: "The next town. I know a place there...not too fancy, but good food. I supposed you're hungry."

"Starved."

"I'm sorry. It's just that, sitting here with you in the car next to me...well, I felt so...wonderful that I didn't think about anything else." He patted her leg. It was an affectionate action, not a pass. But even if it had been a pass, Gale wouldn't have minded.

When the right moment came, she told herself,

putting out the last cigarette, *it would happen.*

A thrill flushed over her nerves at the thought. She looked at the man's even, cleanly cut features. She watched his dark eyes as they kept guard on the road before them. She thought about the soft manly feel of his lips against her own.

Yes, Gale thought, *she wanted him to make love to her. She wanted that more than anything in the world.*

* * * * * * *

Dan watched her intensely as they ate dinner in the small restaurant. He wanted to remember every movement of her face, every action of her hands, her eyes.

He wondered what she thought of him; what she was thinking at that very moment.

"What you thinking?" he suddenly asked.

"Wondering when you'll tell me your plans," she said, amused, her deep blue eyes twinkling.

He smiled. "I didn't really have any plans. I don't really have any now."

"It's a long way back to town, isn't it?" she mused. Her fingers brushed through the long waves of soft blonde hair.

Dan wanted to kiss her hair, her lips, her eyes and cheeks, her neck. He wanted to kiss all of her.

"It's a long way," he admitted, taking another bite of food.

They ate in silence for a little while and then Gale said: "I've never been to Vegas, you know…"

Her eyes invited him to say something.

"Any hurry to look for that job?"

Gale shook her head.

"Well, how about it? Vegas is a long way off—but we *could* get there tonight."

"Aren't you tired driving?"

"Not in the least."

It was settled. They didn't talk throughout the meal, but their eyes communicated silently.

What a lovely, wonderful woman, Dan thought as they walked out to the car.

Then he remembered the filmed scene still in his apartment; a scene which he'd meant to tell Gale about.

And he remembered Holly Hill and what fame and Hollywood had done to her.

Could he give that kind of gift to Gale Ross? What was more important, did he have the right to deny her the opportunity to make her own choice?

As he drove toward Vegas, Dan fought a mental battle that didn't resolve itself. As they reached the outer stretches of the Strip, Dan wondered about another point. *What kind of choice did Gale Ross have?*

He could, possibly, get her a contract, and with her acting ability she would finally make it to the top; if that's what she wanted.

But was it what *he* wanted?

Suddenly Dan realized that regardless of how impossible it was, he could fall in love with Gale Ross—could fall desperately and completely in love with her. He even wondered if it hadn't already happened.

CHAPTER TWENTY-ONE

They had gotten a room in the Sands Hotel. It was a plush suite, with two oversized double beds. The fact that they didn't have any luggage hadn't even been noticed.

Dan watched Gale walk around the room, taking in everything.

"What a place!" she cried, turning, looking at him. "I didn't think they made such places—except in movies."

He grinned, looked at the bottle of champagne the bell-boy had brought up for them.

"I'm glad you like it." He picked up the bottle, struggled for a moment, pressing his thumbs against the cork. A popping sound exploded foam out from the bottle neck. Dan quickly started filling the two glasses.

Gale took one of the glasses, tapped his with it and sipped the champagne. Her eyes were sparkling like starry diamonds.

"I feel embarrassed...having hinted," she finally said. But her expression looked far from embarrassed.

"Forget it. I guess that's where I was subconsciously heading in any case." He touched her arm.

174

It was meant to be merely a gentle touch, affectionate. Nothing more.

An invisible spark seemed to jar them. Dan jerked back, surprised. Like the first time. That first time millions of years before. Or so it seemed.

They stared at each other. Gale shook her head, but her eyes were still dazed as she said: "That's some trick!"

Both of them laughed, happily.

"I bet this place cost a pretty penny," Gale said, sitting down in one of the comfortable yellow chairs opposite the beds.

"Forget it...I brought enough along...and have a check book to match. To say nothing about that ol' plastic card!" He stood over her, looking down, wanting to pull her into his arms, but also wanting to wait for the right moment; the moment when it would just happen so naturally that he wouldn't remember reaching for her.

"You really want to become an actress, don't you, Gale," he said casually, conversationally.

"Almost more than anything else in the world."

Dan thought he heard a slight accent on the "almost," but wasn't sure if it was only his imagination.

"What would you do if you suddenly became a star?" Dan had been thinking a lot, and now the thoughts were jarring into place, one by one. A series of impressions, ideas, mixed lightly with dream-dust. Fantasy; but the kind that could, possibly, come true. But would he have the heart to give that to her? "How important to you is it?"

"What does a woman do with fame? I'd enjoy it, Dan."

175

"No other dreams?"

She studied him, silently, her lips compressing. "Like what?"

"Well, a woman...many women get married, have children...my secretary, Doris, is getting married. She started out wanting to be a big star—gave it up...and now she'd not change a thing..."

Gale frowned slightly. "You letting me down easy?"

"No...just asking questions." He looked away, afraid that the words would come out, the words that would tell her what could possibly be hers. He didn't want to tell her, not right now. "Let's try another subject. I don't want to talk about...business."

"Okay," Gale said in a small voice.

They were silent for a while, sipping the champagne. Dan refilled their glasses.

She was standing next to him, so close it was hard not to touch her. The dress, hugging over her body, showed little of her lush figure, but suggested enough to make it hard not to strip her naked to find out if she was real.

"Want to go out...play the tables?" he inquired.

"What do you think, Dan?" she breathed softly. Her lips, red, moist, half parted, seemed to be waiting.

Then it happened, as it should have happened.

He didn't know how. But she was in his arms, her lips open, hungry under his, her body straining, delightfully supple, throbbing with life and passion and he didn't have to strip her naked to discover how real she was.

The kiss lasted long enough to mix a dizzy red haze with the alcohol in his brain. Without a word,

Dan lifted Gale in his arms, moved to the bed, gently lay her down. He settled next to her, looking into those beautiful eyes, reading a depth of emotion that surprised him.

She certainly couldn't be feeling the same way about him as he was feeling about her.

Gale Ross was an actress with magic. He was, to her, a step towards the top. How could she feel anything other than a cold-blooded need to satisfy his animal desires by giving her body to him?

That should be the only thing that counted.

Dan had known too many hot girls willing to sacrifice their bodies to place themselves in a role. He didn't want another; he didn't want to think that Gale Ross was merely giving herself to him because of what he might do for her career.

Dan started to say something. He felt the words forming on his lips.

No, Gale, you don't have to do this. I'm not working for the studio any longer I can't help your career in that way. You are wasting your time with me.... I'm out of work...don't you understand....?

But their lips were already meeting, hungrily

I'm out of work, and can't do a damned thing for you. Sleep with somebody else. Sleep with Van Houten...sleep with Jack Davis...they'll sign you to a contract so fast your head will spin. And you'll have all that fame...all that glory that was to Holly Hill her death....

And Dan stopped thinking about that, because he didn't want to think any longer, he only wanted to be aware of the curtain of magic now settled between him and the world of reality.

He made love to his woman. He kissed her lips.

He searched over her throbbing white throat. Pulling her dress straps down over the shoulders, he made love to her creamy white flesh. He found her bra, and moved it away so it didn't exist in their fantasy world of romantic love.

He found her breasts, lovely, oval white flesh, dotted with pink, which surged up to meet his lips.

He found her stomach a flat expanse of silken warmth that writhed under his caresses, under his kisses.

I love you, Gale Ross...I love you more than anything in the world.

Then he felt her hands urge him to her. He felt her body arch up, like a dancer, reaching out to him. He felt the velvet heat of her embrace him, and he felt the rhythm tear at his body, at the very center of his being. He heard his own voice whispering in the blackness, heard it whispering over and over again of his love for this woman. This Gale Ross who had come into his life too late; for whom he could do nothing but make love...and love.

Sometime between the awareness of his love and the instant before ecstasy jarred across his nervous system, Dan knew that he would have to tell Gale everything, everything that he knew about her talents, everything that he could make possible for her, by sending her to Jack Davis. He loved her enough to do that much.

* * * * * * *

Gale listened to the voice.

Dan was pacing the room, his hair mussed, his actions jerky, and nervous.

A voice that came out of an agonized man, a voice telling her that she could become a star, if the right people heard about her, if the right people saw that one scene she had done on the *Van Houten* lot. She listened and really didn't feel the excitement his words should have created within her. There were other emotional feelings that were more important. The feeling of wonderful love which had moved every nerve in her mind, body and soul, as Dan Blair had joined their bodies into one ultimate inter-lude of ecstasy a short time before.

That had been all so wonderful. It all clouded over what he was now telling her. He looked ago-nized, desperate. His voice droned on, in a kind of rhythmical confessional mode.

She watched and wanted to put her arms around him, wanted to say it was all right, wanted to let him know that it didn't matter, that nothing really mat-tered.

But she listened, instead, because that was what he wanted.

"You have magic, Gale. You can become a big star. Believe me," he said again. "At first I was afraid to tell you, afraid that it might...what hap-pened to Holly Hill—but that was different. I sud-denly realized that, Gale. I realized that you weren't Holly—and that Holly wasn't like every woman in Hollywood. She was a sex symbol—that's all she could be. You're different...you have talent, looks, and magic. You don't need anything else."

He stood there in the middle of the room, glar-ing at her, his eyes almost tortured.

But all she really cared about was the words he had spoken to her during their moments of love, during their moments of complete, perfect union. Those words were the only ones that counted.

"I do need something else, Dan," she said, standing and moving to his side.

"What else would a woman with your talent need?" he exploded. But his eyes were haunted eyes, pain filled.

"Something more important than mere fame and glamour. Happiness is more important. What you told me about Holly...she never did get happiness. I wouldn't want to take the chance of ending up like her—lonely and unhappy."

Dan looked into her eyes. "You have a great talent, Gale. I know people in Hollywood who would leap at the chance...oh, of course it takes more than talent, hard work...it takes the right promotion, the right direction...a lot of luck, the timing of being at the right place at the right time with the right people backing you..."

He frowned, stood there thoughtful for a moment and then the air slowly sighed out of his chest, past his lips.

"What's wrong with me?" Dan exploded, flinging his arms in the air. "Hell, I have the contacts. The trouble with me is that I've been too fool headed to realize the truth. I don't need to direct...I've never had the experience—but casting...and promoting would be a snap. All you gotta do is have the right contacts. With...with Elliott to do the promotional copy, with Doris to organize the paper work, and with you to Star…what else do we need? Just money! Hell, with Dave Kroph to direct...well, we would get the money...and Dave would jump at the chance of direct!"

He was staring out into blank space. His face was lighted with a glow Gale hadn't seen before. But then, she realized, she hadn't seen very many of his expressions. There was a lot to learn about him.

For a moment longer he stood there, then suddenly moved into action.

Gale merely watched, waited for the right moment to have her say. She couldn't take any second of pleasure away from the man she loved. What she had to say could wait until he was finished. Then she would say it. That would be soon enough.

* * * * * * *

Dan called long distance, Los Angeles. He got Doris Patton on the phone.

Her sleepy voice sounded irritated at first. "Who's calling at this time of night?"

"Dorie, Dan...I have to get hold of Elliott!"

"Dan...Dan, oh, God I'm glad to hear from you. We've been trying to get hold of you for hours. Where are you? What are you doing? What—"

"In Vegas."

"Well, get back. Things have happened since you...disappeared. After you left I got to talking to Dave...he told me about this...Gale Ross, and what a find she was...and then said there was still a negative of the scene. I pointed out what a shame that Dan couldn't have his job back—that finding such a discovery would mean a lot to Murry Van Houten. Dave flipped. He had a quick print made, pushed Murry into a projection booth, said he had to get you back and beg forgiveness to get Gale Ross. Murry flipped when he saw the scene, he ordered

Dave to have you at the studio the next morning. You're back—on your own terms, Dan."

Dan could hardly believe his ears. So simple, so damned simple. And on his own terms. "I'll be back in a few days—do Murry good to sweat!"

He didn't even say good-bye, merely turned and grinned at Gale.

"Honey, you is made!" He plunked the receiver on the hook, told her what Doris had said.

Her face glowed with happiness. But as he took her in his arms, Gale said: "But what if I don't want to be another Holly Hill?"

For a long, frightened moment, Dan hesitated. He looked into her eyes and knew there wasn't anything he wouldn't do for Gale—or wouldn't give up. That puzzled him for a short moment, then he shrugged.

"I thought that was what you wanted."

She shook her head from side to side. "Not *all* I want, Dan. I want to be an actress...but not that way—not at that price!" She gazed deep into his eyes and then her lips smiled, amused.

"Dan, do you remember what you said to me...when we were...making love?" He shook his head, numbly.

She kissed his lips. "If you can remember what it was...while we make love, again...I don't think you'll ever have to ask me that question...or any question about what I want."

Their lips met, warmly, gently, and the magic moved over Dan, a magic that brought memory of a crying voice, sobbing over and over in his head that he loved Gale, that he loved her more than anything else in the world.

When the kiss broke, the words moved past his lips.

"I love you, Gale. Oh, how I love you!"

Her eyes twinkled brightly. She tensed against him, and whispered in his ears. "I'm glad you remembered, my love...my dear, dear love, I love you, too..."

They kissed again, but this time it was only the beginning, not for a moment, but for a lifetime. A lifetime filled with fame, glamour, and the one important ingredient that made success the rewarding thing it should be: love.

But he wasn't thinking about that after the first kiss, he wasn't thinking about anything except the wonderful thrill of being near the woman he loved, touching her, loving her eyes, her lips, her throat, her breasts. Loving all there was to love in his woman, his Gale Ross.

ABOUT THE AUTHOR

Charles Nuetzel was born in San Francisco in 1934, and writes:

"As long as I can remember I wanted to be a writer. It was a dream I never thought would materialize. But with the help of Forrest J Ackerman, who became my agent, I managed to finally make it into print.

"I was lucky enough not only in selling my work to publishers but also ending up packaging books for some of them, and finally becoming a 'publisher' much like those who had bought my first novels. From there it as a simple leap to editing not only a sci-fi anthology, but a line of sci-fi books for Powell Sci-Fi back in the 1960s. Throughout these active professional years I had the chance to design some covers and do graphic cover layouts for pocket books & magazines."

Much of his work in covers and graphics are a result of having had a father who was a professional commercial artist, and who did a number of covers for sci-fi magazines in the 1950s and later for pocket books—even for some of Mr. Nuetzel's books.

In retirement he has become involved in swing dancing, a long time lover of Big Band jazz. But more interestingly world travels have taken him (and his wife Brigitte) across the world, to Hawaii, Caribbean, Mexico, Kenya, Egypt, Peru, having a lifelong interest in ancient civilizations. His website is full of thousands of pictures taken during these trips.

www.ingramcontent.com/pod-product-compliance
Lightning Source LLC
Chambersburg PA
CBHW032011240626

47153CB00003B/1213